WINTER'S TRUTH

(Heat of Love bonus novella)

BY LETA BLAKE

An Original Publication from Leta Blake Books

Winter's Truth
Written and published by Leta Blake
Cover by Dar Albert
Formatted by BB eBooks

Other Books by Leta Blake

Contemporary

Will & Patrick Wake Up Married
Will & Patrick's Endless Honeymoon
Cowboy Seeks Husband
The Difference Between
Bring on Forever
Stay Lucky

Sports

The River Leith

The Training Season Series
Training Season
Training Complex

Musicians

Smoky Mountain Dreams
Vespertine

New Adult

Punching the V-Card

'90s Coming of Age Series
Pictures of You
You Are Not Me
Only You

Winter Holidays

North's Pole

The Mr. Christmas Series
Mr. Frosty Pants
Mr. Naughty List
Mr. Jingle Bells

A Boy for All Seasons
My December Daddy

Fantasy

Any Given Lifetime

Reimagined Fairy Tales

Flight
Levity

Paranormal & Shifters

Angel Undone
Omega Mine

Horror

Raise Up Heart

Omegaverse

Heat of Love Series
White Heat
Slow Heat
Alpha Heat
Slow Birth
Bitter Heat

For Sale Series
Heat for Sale
Bully for Sale

Audiobooks
letablake.com/audiobooks

Discover more about the author online

Leta Blake
letablake.com

Acknowledgements

Thank you to the following people: Mom and Dad, Brian and Cecily. All the wonderful members of my Patreon who inspire, support, and advise me. Keira Andrews for constant cheerleading. Devon Vesper for the amazing editing work. Dar Albert for the gorgeous cover. And thank you to my readers who make it all worthwhile.

About the Book

Winter-fox brings Viro some surprising truths for the holiday

Viro Sabel is eleven years old and still entirely innocent about life. This year winter-fox brings him some surprising truths that alter the way he sees the world and his place in it.

Learn more about the character of Viro, *Slow Heat*'s Vale and Jason's son, in this **winter holiday-themed novella**. This medium-sized bonus book features spicy scenes between Vale and Jason, family scenes, and emotional moments. While the novella's epilogue teases a relationship for an adult Viro, it ends with a mystery regarding this person's identity.

This story is ***not* a standalone** and is best read as an addition to the *Heat of Love* series, preferably after reading *Slow Heat*, *Alpha Heat*, and *Slow Birth*. But if you should happen to read it out of order, you can find the rest of the books in the series here:

SLOW HEAT
ALPHA HEAT
BITTER HEAT
SLOW BIRTH
WINTER'S HEART

Dedication

Dedicated to my patrons at Patreon who support the business end of making books and audiobooks. Thank you to the fans of the *Heat of Love* universe! This bonus story is also for you!

CHAPTER ONE
VALE

VALE HADN'T BEEN alone in his study for very long when the door creaked open, and his son's dark head appeared around the edge of the wood along with the side of his pale face and the shadow of his dark lashes.

"Pater?" Viro asked, staying just at the threshold, waiting for an invitation inside just as Vale had instructed him to do long ago during his toddler days. His voice was firm and somber. Not unusual for his and Jason's serious son. At eleven, Viro—Ro for short—was full of questions and unearned confidence. Vale suspected Ro would present as an alpha when the time came—and it could come any day. The dominant energy in him was quite strong.

"Pater? I have a question," Ro called into the room.

Vale looked up from the poem he'd been toying with. "Yes, my love?" He could tell by the way the door nearly vibrated with Ro's restrained energy that his son was struggling not to barge in, but his feet stayed outside the threshold.

Ro's head ducked back from view. His voice came disembodied from the doorway. "Winter-fox isn't real, is he?"

Vale glanced out the windows of his study, toward the garden where Jason was hard at work draping garlands along the top of the fence and adding glittery bulbs to the bushes and trees.

Every year Jason went overboard with Feast of Winter's Heart decorations, and every year Vale indulged Jason's enthusiasm with a devastating fondness. Truly, it was endlessly mortifying to still be so besotted with his alpha. Though since they were *Érosgápe*—mates chosen by wolf-god to be together and granted the most obsessive and purest of love—most would claim it would have been utterly *unnatural* if Vale didn't adore him.

Still, their age difference was stark, and Vale had assumed, despite Jason's assurances, that eventually it would get in the way. But Jason had never used being younger as an excuse to do less than his best. He worked hard at everything he did. He strove to be the best alpha, the best father, and the best at his work. Vale thought Jason was, in fact, the best human being alive, and it was terribly endearing how his earnestness hadn't faded away along with his once-terrifying youth.

Jason was still far too many years younger than Vale by society's standards. But *Érosgápe* were *Érosgápe*, and Jason's youth was something Vale had long ago made his peace with. Indeed, it was something he now cherished when in the throes of a ferocious heat. Jason could always keep up with Vale's needs, even when he was wild with them.

"Pater?" Ro said again, this time rattling the doorknob impatiently. "Winter-fox is a lie, *isn't he?*"

Vale sighed.

Jason would be so disappointed. The Feast of Winter's Heart was the holiday wherein wolf-god's younger brother, a magical winter-fox, was lured into homes by beautiful decorations and the ringing of bells. In exchange for being invited to a feast, he left presents behind for the children. The joy of it was already so short-lived, only possible for a handful of years in any family's life. Once Ro no longer believed…well, that would be the end of winter-fox's visits. That was the way of it and always had been.

"Pater!" Ro demanded, making the door creak. "Answer me!"

Vale slid his unfinished poem into his desk drawer and turned the lock. The poem was nothing serious or deep, not like some of the more radical material from his youth. Still, it was definitely sexual and entirely about the activities he and Jason had gotten up to the night before. Nothing appropriate for eleven-year-old eyes.

That accomplished, he cleared his throat and called, "Why don't you come in so we can talk?"

Ro didn't hesitate, bursting into the often-forbidden room. His dark head whipped back and forth between the windows and the fireplace, taking it all in again. He nodded in satisfaction to find it all the same as it ever was, as he stretched his ever-growing legs by walking around Vale's sacred space. "I like it in here."

Vale almost felt guilty about not allowing Ro access to his sanctuary more often, but as their son had grown, he'd become more and more dominant, taking over more and more of their lives. The high level of attachment wasn't one-sided in the least. Neither Jason nor Vale enjoyed leaving Ro for any length of time even though they knew he was in perfectly good hands with Miner and Yule—Jason's parents—or with their friends, Rosen and Yosef. Still, they missed him so much when they were away, and, unfortunately, they had to be separated from their son far too often in order to deal with Vale's unpredictable heats.

Knowing Ro was the only child they could ever have had always made their son's every smile and laugh beyond precious to them both. For his part, Jason couldn't say no to anything Ro asked for, and Vale couldn't claim to be much stricter. There was no doubt they'd spoiled him terribly, and for that reason, perhaps, Ro was very immature for his age. That spoiling was undoubtedly where all Ro's unearned confidence came from, too.

But overall, he was a good child. Warm, honest, and funny. He was an ally to outcasts at school and always stood up for what was right. He had a strong moral compass and abhorred lies. He wanted everyone to live by the same code of ethics he did.

Yes, Vale was certain Ro would be an alpha.

Given all they *did* allow Ro access to within their home and outside it, the study was the one place Vale tried to keep just for himself. And sometimes for Jason. Such as when they wanted to be alone as *Érosgápe* mates, naked and trembling and loving each other… *Then*, they'd sneak into the study and lock the door behind them just in case.

Vale shivered at the memories of all that he and Jason had done in this room over the years. So much pleasure, so much joy, so much love.

Wolf-god, where was his mind? Was another heat coming on so soon? He'd only just had one a month ago.

Still, Vale sensed the quiver deep inside, the shivery-hot sensation that heralded the intense waves of need. He'd been entirely too horny for his own good the last two days, too. The so-called change of life—when heats began to twist and morph with aging hormones—was hitting him harder than any other omegas he knew. It was frustrating and scary to have heat after heat coming at him with so little time between. Thankfully he had Jason to reassure him. But it didn't mean he wasn't afraid for the future.

Vale shook himself from his worries and turned his attention to his son, who was still strolling around the room like he owned it. "Let's sit on the sofa."

"Okay—Pater, what's this?" Ro asked, waylaid by his curiosity as he headed toward the leather couch. His long finger trailed over the dusty lid to a heart-shaped box resting on a small table next to one of Vale's bookshelves. Normally Vale kept the box higher up, a precaution from Ro's younger days, but he'd taken it down a week ago so he could reach a book behind it, and he'd never put it back.

Vale crossed the room and touched the box, too, remembering his old friend. "That's Zephyr."

Ro had been quite young when Vale's silver cat had died. She'd been such a bratty, opinionated, wonderful friend to Vale during some of the loneliest years of his life. Tears pricked even now when he remembered her.

Sweet memories of her sleeping next to a newborn Ro came to mind. Both of them on the little purple blanket Yosef and Rosen had gifted, spread out before the fire. Ah, Zephyr had been so peaceful and protective back then, staying close to the baby while Vale had obsessed over his son's tiny form, terrified that Ro might stop breathing if left unobserved for even a single moment. The ecstasy of parenthood had consumed Vale's mind back then, rather the way heat worries did now.

"Zephyr. Your cat," Ro said, running his fingertip along the edge of the heart and tilting his head with a sweet smile.

"Do you remember her at all?"

"No, but I know you loved her." Ro's eyebrows twitched up. "Was she a very small cat?" He lifted the box to examine the bottom.

Vale took it from his hands. "She's been cremated." Vale lifted the box high up on the bookshelf again. "This holds her ashes."

"Oh, you burned her up." Ro gave a wise nod, still gazing up at the box. "I see now."

"Well, the crematory handled the burning," Vale said, knowing how Ro's imagination could take flight sometimes. "It's not as though I did it myself in the fireplace."

Ro looked toward the hearth with some interest, as if he were imagining that possibility, and then he nodded again. "Good choice, Pater. That would have been too gruesome by far." He put his hand over his heart as if it hurt to consider this flight of morbid fancy.

Vale took hold of Ro's shoulder and guided him over to the leather sofa. The sofa

Vale had been fucked on so, so, so many times. So many *wonderful* times.

Vale winced. Wolf-god in heaven, this level of baseline arousal only meant one thing.

With a grimace, Vale fought the prickling beneath his skin. Surely, he had a few more days left? Certainly? He bit into his lip and willed his mind to focus and his body to behave. With any luck, this was just a hot flash, a sensation many omegas suffered as their bodies wound down from their fertile years. Many of his omega friends said it felt similar to an oncoming heat.

"Pater, I want you to tell me the truth," Ro said, lifting his sharp chin as he plopped down onto the sofa and gazed up at Vale seriously. "Is winter-fox real? Yes or no?"

Vale sat beside his son, taking a moment to answer. "Well, let's think about this carefully." The hot prickles ebbed away, and his mind cleared. "You know that winter-fox only visits little children—"

"I'm not little. I'm eleven."

"You are, and your father and I are very aware of just how big you're getting."

"Then you know I'm way too big for baby stuff like winter-fox, and you should just tell me the truth."

Vale tilted his head. "Think about it carefully, though, Ro. Winter-fox only comes if a child believes."

"But is he real?"

"Winter-fox is real, yes."

Ro gritted his teeth. "Why are you lying? You know I hate lies."

"I'm not lying."

"You are! I'm eleven years old! I know winter-fox is a lie! I know it's you and Father leaving the presents!"

Vale sighed and kept his voice as calm as possible as he answered. "I'm not lying, Ro. Winter-fox *is* real. Well, the spirit of winter-fox is real. Winter-fox is meant to instill a sense of magic, hope, joy, and love into the darkest nights of the year. All that remains true, even if winter-fox himself is just a story."

"Hmmph," Ro said, crossing his arms over his chest. "I knew it."

"Well, you're getting smarter every day." Vale touched Ro's dark hair, smoothing his fingers through it and marveling at what a mixture his son was of himself and Jason physically. He had his own fair skin and dark hair, but Jason's blue eyes and, if the number of times they'd had to buy new pants in the last year was any indication, Jason's height, too. He also had something of Miner, Jason's pater, about his jawline, which was nice. But Vale was also deeply grateful to see evidence of his own long-dead parents in the shape of Ro's fingers and nose.

Vale cleared his throat and turned to gaze out the window again at Jason at work bedecking the garden. "You didn't say anything to your father about this before coming to me?"

Usually, Ro liked to help Jason decorate

for the holiday, and it was strange for him to be inside instead of outside stringing up bows and shiny ornaments with Jason now.

"No," Ro's lips lifted in a soft, disdainful sneer. "We should stop him. I don't see any point in decorating if winter-fox is a lie."

"Mmm. Why does Father think you aren't helping him?"

Ro blew out an annoyed breath. "I don't know. I came looking for you when he started pulling out the boxes." He leaned around Vale to peer out the window. "Maybe he thinks I went to the bathroom?"

Vale laughed softly. "Maybe. But why didn't you ask your father about winter-fox?"

Ro rolled his eyes. "He wants me to stay a baby."

"So you think *he* would have lied to you about winter-fox just being a story?" Vale smiled at that. Jason was always sincere and earnest. Lying was not his baby alpha's forte any more than it was their son's. He probably wouldn't have hesitated in his honesty, unlike Vale.

"Yes. He'd *lie*," Ro asserted. "And then try to trick me into believing again. Like when he left those fake fox pawprints in the snow last year." Ro re-crossed his arms over his chest in the opposite direction to emphasize his irritation with his father. He leaned back against the sofa, rolling his eyes. "I can't believe I fell for that. I was such a baby then."

"Well, they were very convincing pawprints." Jason had had so much fun making them, certain it would extend the years of Ro's belief in winter-fox's magic. Oh well.

Ro snorted.

"You're our only son, and—" Vale started, and Ro groaned.

"I know, but I can't stay little forever, Pater! And I don't *believe* in winter-fox. So we *can't* celebrate. That's that." He said it with such finality that Vale's heart panged.

"It doesn't have to be that way."

"Yes, it does."

Vale ignored the surge of prickling heat that rose in him again. "No, it doesn't. We could have one last Feast of Winter's Heart as a family."

It wasn't just Jason who would be disappointed if they canceled at the last minute like this. Miner and Yule, Jason's parents, would be upset, too. They loved the feast and had only been able to enjoy it with Jason for a few years of his youth before his belief in winter-fox was spoiled by his friend Xan. If Ro insisted on not believing now, the entire family would be sad.

"What? And lie to Father?" Ro shook his head. "I don't tell lies."

"We don't have to lie to him. We just won't tell him you know. Withholding information isn't quite the same as lying."

Ro's eyebrow popped up sharply. "No."

"Ro, think of it like this. The spirit behind the story of winter-fox is one of giving, isn't it? What better gift for your father, grandfather, and grandpater than one last Feast of Winter's Heart for them and one last visit from winter-fox for you? Afterward, I could tell them that this year will be the last, so that they won't be so disappointed next year."

Ro chewed on his lower lip. "I don't know."

"Don't you want to celebrate one more time? Won't you miss it?" Vale knew it wasn't right to be so manipulative, but the thought of Jason's expression if Ro were to march out there right now and declare, "Stop decorating, Father, I know the truth about winter-fox," was just too painful to consider. Vale couldn't endure Jason's unhappiness. Not if he had any way of preventing it.

"I guess I *will* miss it," Ro agreed. "I like getting presents. But it's wrong, isn't it? To keep on celebrating even after I know? It's not how it's meant to be. Bad things will happen."

"Darling, that's a superstition."

"Is it?" Ro pondered. "It says in the Holy Book of Wolf that the Feast of Winter's Heart should only be celebrated by true believers. I read it in bed last night myself."

"Darling…"

"Celebrating when I'm not a believer anymore…" Ro's dark eyebrows furrowed. "Isn't it like trying to trick wolf-god?"

"Not really." Vale knew he probably shouldn't be encouraging Ro to go against his highly developed sense of right and wrong, but what real harm could a final celebration do? "Ro, love…" Vale paused before pulling out the final stop. "We've already bought your presents, you realize?"

Ro's eyes brightened with interest.

"All the things you listed? Your father got them for you. But if 'winter-fox' can't bring them to you, I suppose we should donate them to a family with a child who still believes."

Ro gasped and sat upright. "That's mean!"

"Yes," Vale agreed.

It really was. He'd always wondered if he was a selfish parent, and, as Ro aged, it seemed more and more likely that was the case. Though Jason would deny it and say Vale was the best pater in the world. Ridiculous and sweet, and absolutely blinded by *Érosgápe* love.

"Why would you be so mean?"

"Because it's also mean to steal the Feast of Winter's Heart away from your father and grandparents while still expecting to get the presents, isn't it?"

"You could save them for my birthday!"

Vale shrugged. "I could. But do you really want to wait that long?"

Ro frowned, thinking hard. "I won't have to lie? Really?"

"Just go along with things. Easy as that. You know how your father is, he'll be so excited himself, he won't notice anything is different. So long as you don't outright confess what you know, he'll be willing to think you still believe."

Ro squirmed. "But doesn't it go against what winter-fox is *all about* if I get presents when I know he isn't real?"

"He *is* real."

"Right, he's 'real' because the 'spirit' is real. I don't know." Ro's mind was clearly churning. "Is it in the *spirit* of the spirit to get presents when I'm not supposed to?"

"It's whatever it is, darling."

"Won't wolf-god be angry?"

"You don't believe in winter-fox, but you believe in wolf-god?"

Ro's eyes went wide. "Don't *you*?"

Vale cleared his throat and spoke carefully. "I think there are many beautiful stories that impart important messages about life, and the story of wolf-god is—"

"Absolutely real!" Ro cut him off fervently. "Grandpater says so!"

"Oh, well, if Miner says so, then I suppose it *is* so," Vale said and tried to keep the sarcasm from his voice.

His envy of Ro's relationship with his grandpater wasn't generous, especially with Miner so sick these days. *Of course*, Miner had turned to religion for comfort. Nearly everyone in his situation would.

"Grandpater doesn't lie," Ro said firmly. "Never, ever, ever."

"All right," Vale agreed, though he wasn't sure if it was wise to let Ro hold any human being, much less one as fallible as Miner Hoff, in such high esteem.

But it brought Miner so much joy to have Ro in his life. Vale would never want to come between them. Especially not now, when there wasn't enough time left anymore to be petty, not when it came to love.

A hot sizzle of heat pulsed through his veins, and Vale gasped softly.

"What's wrong, Pater?" Ro asked, his blue eyes growing concerned.

Vale fanned himself with his hand and then rose from the sofa. "I'm just overheated. I'll open a window. Run off and help your father decorate. And remember, go along with things, Ro. You don't have to lie. Just enjoy your last year as a child, and let your father enjoy it, too."

"All right," Ro said doubtfully. He caught hold of Vale just as he was about to open the window. He pressed his forehead against Vale's shoulder. "Pater, I love you. Don't be sick like grandpater."

"Oh, love," Vale said, hugging Ro tight. "I'm not sick. I promise." He dropped a kiss on Ro's soft hair.

"You're just too hot," Ro affirmed, squeezing tighter.

"Yes, it's just the heat from the fire," Vale whispered, tugging Ro's arms free and turning to the windows, pulling them open to let in the winter-cold air.

Ro glanced toward the fireplace, empty of flames but still glowing with banked coals from the morning and frowned again.

"Go help your father, love. Have fun."

Ro squeezed him and left the room.

Vale breathed in and out slowly, gripping the windowsill where Jason had once reached through to take a fabric bookmark from him, and on another occasion, jerked off all over Vale's chest as he'd knelt on the floor inside. Oh, those early days of need and yearning. They were so beautiful to remember.

Slick released, wetting his hole.

"Give me a week," Vale pleaded, praying to a wolf-god he personally wasn't sure was anything more than a pretty story. "A week for this final Feast of Winter's Heart with my son. And then I'll go through it again. All I need is one week."

Prayer had never helped ward off a heat before.

Vale tried not to resent his unpredictable heats, but it was hard. They'd prevented him from ever returning to teaching after Ro's birth, and they'd kept Vale always vulnerable and nervous in a way he disliked. At least Jason had the stamina and youth to deal with Vale's pre-heat urges and the long days of heat themselves. He couldn't imagine going through this indignity with an older alpha as his mate.

Jason looked up from where he was draping tinsel over the shrubs. He scented the air and turned toward where Vale stood. A smirk grew on Jason's face before spreading into a full-fledged smile. "Is that slick for me?" he called.

Vale's knees trembled, and his cock thickened. Even more slick released. He ached to be fucked long and hard. "Yes."

Jason started toward him, licking his lips. "As I seem to recall, that window is just the right height to—"

"Father! I'm here to help!" Ro shouted, running through the garden, red cap thrown over his dark hair and a silver-threaded coat pulled on to keep him warm. It hadn't snowed yet, but there was some indication it might start that night.

Jason shot Vale a look which promised he'd get what he needed later. Probably once

Ro was asleep. But that didn't solve Vale's problem now. His hole trembled with want, and his cock was rigid with lust. Even his nipples ached.

Vale took another slow breath of the cold air and then shut the window again. He headed upstairs to their bathroom, retrieving from its hiding place in the back of the closet the thick alpha dildo Jason used during heats when he needed a short break. With the door locked, Vale got naked and took matters into his own hands. His hole was so wet he didn't need any lubrication as he pressed the fat dildo inside and groaned in relief.

With his legs spread and his eyes closed, he leaned against the bathroom counter with one hand and worked the dildo quickly with the other. He could almost imagine it was Jason inside him, except for the absence of his warmth along his back, the dearth of dirty nothings whispered in his ear, and the lack of a sweetly perfect cock rubbing *all* the right places. It took far too long, but he finally reached climax. The hot thrum under his skin retreated.

In the aftermath, clarity descended once more. If the stinging dissatisfaction in his bones was any indication, wolf-god planned to ignore his plea. As he always had. Frustrated and disappointed, Vale began to plan. If wolf-god didn't grant him a week's reprieve, if the threatening heat crested and crashed over him before they could celebrate Ro's last Feast of Winter's Heart, they'd need to arrange help and quickly.

Vale gritted his teeth as he cleaned the dildo and put it back in its hiding spot. He showered and dressed again, trailing to the window to look down at the decorated garden below and watch his two beloveds laughing as they festooned it more fully. Wolf-god, why did his body constantly betray him? He'd lost so much over the years to the brutality of heats. It was beyond unfair that he'd lose this last winter holiday with his son as well.

If wolf-god is busy, then I beg you as his brother, winter-fox, bring me a reprieve for Jason and Ro's sake, Vale prayed again.

But he knew winter-fox was just a story, and even if he wasn't, Ro no longer believed. There would be no gifts from winter-fox this year.

CHAPTER TWO

JASON

"**O**H, FUCK, YES," Jason said, sliding into Vale's hot body and collapsing against his chest. Vale's hard cock pressed against his stomach and his firm, hairy legs drew up against the sides of his chest. "Baby, you're soaked for me."

"Ungh," was Vale's only response. His body convulsed beneath Jason with a shuddery, preliminary anal orgasm that left Jason hornier than when he'd still been outside of Vale and aching to be in.

The door to their bedroom was locked, and Ro had been sound asleep when they'd moved their activities from the safety of Vale's study up to their room. Wolf-god, it was already so good. Soft mattress, soft sheets, and Vale's open body taking his cock like he was made for it.

Because he *had* been made for it. They were *Érosgápe*. Destined mates. Pre-ordained lovers. Their pleasure was hotter, brighter, and more intense than any other lovers'. Their orgasms were perfect. Their love divine. Fucking Vale was better than anything in wolf-god's own heaven.

Jason bent to suck on one of Vale's nipples, chuckling as Vale convulsed again, his body sensitive to Jason's every touch. He knew he could make Vale come from just this, too, and it was a powerful feeling. Red-cheeked and eyes glazed over with over-wrought passion, Vale was a dream to behold. Jason stared down at his beloved, fucking into his body with strong, easy strokes. Sheer bliss. There was nothing better.

Vale's breath hitched, and he twisted

under Jason, softening even more, opening to him with a wet surge of heat around his cock.

"I love you," Jason reassured Vale, as he gasped and whined, a hint of confusion in his eyes as he succumbed to his pleasure even more deeply. "Mm, you are delicious," Jason praised. "You are *perfect* on my cock."

Vale's green eyes sparked with hotter lust. He gripped his own knees, holding them back further, and went still beneath Jason, a signal indicating he wanted Jason to lose control, to fuck him as hard as he could. It also meant Vale would soon grow very, *very* loud. Jason glanced over his shoulder to double-check the door. Definitely locked.

"What if he wakes up?"

Vale didn't answer. He squirmed on Jason's cock, and another gush of liquid heat rushed over Jason's balls, wetting the sheets beneath them.

"Oh, baby," Jason said, taking Vale's chin in hand, momentarily missing the beard Vale had always worn until the gray in it had begun to irritate his vanity. "You need it, don't you? You need my knot?"

Vale's response was an immediate and powerful orgasm. He cried out as a full-on cock-spurting, body-shaking climax took him over, along with wet anal convulsions that gripped Jason's cock hard in Vale's muscular, omega asshole. So perfect. So beautiful. So ready for a knot.

"Fuck," Jason said, his nipples tightening and his balls drawing up snug. "Vale, baby? I think your heat is coming," he said softly. But Vale was still gone in pleasure, his hips moving up to catch Jason's plunging cock, and his eyes wild with need.

Jason kissed Vale's tender mouth, pouring his passion into it. A roaring lust for Vale gone sex-mad in heat consumed him. He was eager for it, though they'd just shared the holy communion a month ago. Still…

The thrill of knotting his omega, of spending days dedicated solely to indulging in pleasure and deepening their connection.

Coddling every wish and whim, devouring Vale shamelessly, hungrily, over and over again. Jason's heart pounded with anticipation. So what if the timing wasn't convenient? Heat was heat. It came when it came, and there was no stopping it—no matter how many times Vale had tried.

Oh, baby, Jason thought, kissing Vale's mouth again. *You never learn.*

Vale must have known over dinner. Must have known earlier in the day when the scent of his slick had wafted over the garden. Must have known as Jason had licked his hole until he'd cried in the study. And yet, he'd said nothing. Because of the feast. Because of their son.

Probably, also, because of him.

But that didn't matter now. What mattered was satisfying Vale enough tonight that they could talk through a plan in the morning. Assuming the heat hadn't arrived fully by then. The way Vale fell apart with each of Jason's thrusts made it clear the heat was roaring in fast.

Jason plowed into Vale with a rough, steady tempo, paying attention for any sign of his knot. As Vale shattered again and again, Jason held strong, keeping his own orgasm at bay. And when he did finally climax, it came as a relief that he felt no urge to knot. The heat pheromones hadn't entirely engaged yet. They had a little time.

Despite having just made love, it was evident Vale still needed more. He squirmed and begged, whimpering with blind need. Without the heat pheromones to entice Jason to hardness again, he was left with little choice but to satisfy his grunting, pleading, aching omega with his fist. They'd grown used to fisting over the years, and Vale took Jason's hand almost as easily as he took his dick these days. With kisses to Vale's hips and thighs, Jason positioned himself to best breach Vale with his hand. As he did, Vale shivered with pleasure and whispered dazed words of praise.

Jason fucked his hand in and out of Vale's hole slowly, bringing him to a state of bliss. Over and over, Vale broke with pleasure, like the heat was already on him, until he *finally* exploded with cum, slick, and a cry that shook Jason to the quick.

Carefully withdrawing his hand from Vale's limp body, and after checking the Vale was all right, Jason went to the bathroom to wash up. He brought a warm washcloth with him when he returned, and before he'd finished wiping a delirious Vale clean with a warm, damp towel, his sweet omega had passed out asleep, finally satisfied.

But, Jason saw, still sporting an erection. Oh, yes, the heat was coming, and it wouldn't wait.

Tomorrow would be the first full day. Jason was sure of it.

At least Ro still believed in winter-fox. There was always next year for the feast. For now, he had his *Érosgápe's* heat to handle. There was nothing more beautiful in his entire world than sharing that intimacy and knotting deep inside of Vale's needy body.

Kissing Vale's warm cheek, he smiled.

Nothing at all.

"MY HEAT IS coming."

Jason rolled over, his cock already hard from the scent of Vale's heavy slick, and his eyes still crusted with sleep after their long, hard fuck the night before. "I know."

Vale's shoulders rounded, and the light from the window streamed over his back, highlighting his shoulder blades like sharp, white wings. "I'm sorry."

"Baby, being with you during heat is one of the highlights of my life," Jason reminded him. "Why are you apologizing?"

"Because it keeps happening so often."

"The greatest bliss a couple can know," Jason said, sliding a hand down Vale's back and tugging him to face him. "The highest form of intimacy."

He guided Vale over his hips, groaning lightly as Vale slid down onto his hard cock. He smirked as Vale quivered around him, tensing and releasing around the firmness of Jason's dick.

"The most divine experience of sexual and spiritual union." He lifted his hips to grind into Vale, making them both pant. "Poor me."

"Yes, poor you," Vale said, his cock flexing against his stomach and welling with pre-come. "It's considered so divine because it's only supposed to happen once every six months or so, and for many omegas at my age only once a year, sometimes less often even than that. But for me…it's the opposite. This is our third heat in just half a year." Vale choked on tears, and Jason reached up to wipe at his wet cheeks. "I love being with you, Jason, but…it's cruel, isn't it?"

"Cruel?" Jason pulled Vale down to his

chest, staying buried inside but not thrusting. Just holding him close and trying to comfort his crying omega. "How is this cruel?"

"How *isn't* it?" Vale asked urgently. "To have it happen again and again when we can't even do the thing it's meant for? When we can't make another child together?" His voice cracked with sadness. "I want so much to have your knot mean more than just pleasure."

"You say pleasure like it's a sin." Jason lifted his hips again to show how not-sinful their pleasure was, and Vale's body took his thrust easily. The hot walls of his ass worked Jason's length, and Vale's eyes rolled up slightly before he caught his breath and pinched one of Jason's nipples hard.

"Stop."

Stilling, Jason gripped Vale's hips and held him in place. "I love the pleasure we make."

"I know. But I want your children, Jason," Vale said quietly. "And not just one child. Every heat, it gets more intense, this desire to be filled with your baby. To be the omega who takes your seed and makes it flesh. I can't seem to make peace with it. It breaks my heart."

"I know."

And he did know, even though he didn't feel the same sense of urgency, probably because of his relative youth, there was no doubt that mid-heat it took everything in him not to remove the condom at Vale's fevered urgings, plunge inside him, and join their bodies into new flesh. Create a new child, a sign of their perfection and wolf-god's blessing on their union. But, in the end, all he really wanted was Vale's health and happiness. All he needed was Vale by his side.

"You want it, too?" Vale's eyes widened, and Jason swore he felt Vale's pulse thump against his cock.

"Not the way you do," Jason said. "I just want you. Ro is enough for us. He was a miracle. But you are my greatest joy, my heart, my life." He pulled Vale harder against his hips, pushing up into his body, adoring the sweet, hot velvet of his *Érosgápe's* body gripping him. "And being with you, helping you with heat, knotting you, is the best part of my life."

Vale closed his eyes. "You deserve more children. You're a good father."

"I don't need more children. It's enough to see you with Ro. You're a good pater."

"I'm not," Vale said, shaking his head. His cock stood hard between them, and Jason was tempted to hump up against it but held back. He knew Vale was easily swayed away from serious conversations with sex, but he also knew Vale would resent not being able to say all of this now before the heat set in. "I'm not a *terrible* pater, but I'm not very good at it either. Not like Miner."

"Vale—"

"I have to work at it. But you're a natural father, and Miner is a natural pater."

"Ro adores you."

"Not as much as he adores Miner."

Jason scoffed. "My pater doesn't have to discipline him. You're his parent. He'll always love you—"

"I know," Vale cut him off. "I *do* know. Let's not go down that path now. My petty jealousy isn't as important as the question of what we need to do about this heat." He thrust his hips down, and hot pre-come smeared over Jason's abs.

"We can send Ro to my parents' house."

Vale clenched around Jason. "But this will be his last Feast of Winter's Heart!"

"Will it?" Jason cocked his head, thinking. "My last one was at six, but that was Xan's fault. Or his brother Ray's really for telling *him*. Besides, Ro is still so innocent."

"He's not always the quickest at grabbing concepts, no," Vale agreed.

"Surely, we can get one more year out of him then. I can put the fox prints out again."

Vale shook his head. "This will be his

last." He groaned. "Wolf-god, why? I can't go into heat now."

"Vale," Jason said seriously, taking Vale's hands in his own and kissing them as he slowly, firmly thrust up into his body. Vale's head fell back, exposing his throat as he groaned. "Your heat *is* coming. If it holds off an entire day, we'll be lucky. Feel how wet you are for me. Feel how soft you are, opening up for my cock. Your womb will descend soon. Remember the heat that brought Ro to us? There was no warning at all. At least we know in advance for this one."

Vale's lips quivered, and he shifted, jolting as Jason's cock pressed against his internal glands. "Oh," he whimpered. "You're going to make me come."

"I love making you come."

Vale sighed, stilling against Jason and begging, "Please give me a moment. Don't move."

Jason held very still, but he could feel in Vale's body how close he was to giving in and riding Jason's cock with abandon. His neck was flushed, his cheeks, too, and his belly moved with tight, taut breaths. They would share an orgasm very shortly.

Vale whispered, "I thought I wanted this last year of winter-fox for your sake, but now I see I wanted it, too." Vale shuddered and covered his face. His voice was thready as he continued, "You'll have to let your parents know. Oh, wolf-god, Jason. I need to come now, darling. Help me."

Jason flipped Vale onto his back, plowing into him with hard, long strokes, covering Vale's mouth with his hand as he fucked the shouts from his beloved's shaking body. When it was over, slick and come all over their bodies and on the sheets, Vale lay back on the bed with his fingers sliding in and out of his hole, eyes still glazed with lust.

Jason washed in the bathroom and tied on his favorite red robe. He was ready to head downstairs when Vale called out to him.

"Yes?" Jason came to sit on the bed next

to Vale's naked form and stroked a hand over Vale's morning-stubbled cheek. "I need to call my parents and check on Ro."

Vale kissed his palm before leaning back, raising his legs, and gripping the back of his knees. He held himself open, exposing the wet beauty of his asshole. "I know, but fist me first? I already feel like I'm going out of my mind."

Jason glanced at the clock. Ro would wake before long, but Vale was in no state to see the boy. Not until he'd had his need satisfied, and probably not even then. The first real heat wave was so close to descending.

"All right," he said, discarding his robe, knowing his cock wasn't going to settle for just watching his hand get inside Vale's sweet body. "I'll fist you again."

Vale sighed with pleasure and rested his head on the pillow, open and waiting.

Heart pounding, Jason reached into the bedside table to get out the alpha condoms he only used when necessary. It wouldn't do for Vale's heat to come on mid-fuck, triggering his womb to descend and open while Jason was still inside, risking pregnancy. He could already feel the changes in his reaction to Vale since their first encounter this morning, and he sensed it was possible to knot him now.

"Let me kiss it first."

Vale's soft cry of pleasure as Jason pressed his tongue inside and tasted the sweetness of his omega's slick drove all worry about anything other than his *Érosgápe's* pleasure out of his mind. Five minutes later, Vale rode Jason's fist like a wild thing, and ten minutes after that, he threw his hips back, catching Jason's slamming cock, as they fucked like dogs. It was beautiful and intense and a harbinger of what was to come.

When Jason shot into the condom, he felt a tingle at the base of his cock, and he braced himself for the knot, but luckily it didn't swell and lock him inside just yet. He nuzzled Vale's sweaty neck, pulling out and heading back into the bathroom to clean up again.

Afterward, as Jason pulled on his loose pants and his robe again, he studied Vale passed out on the bed, sleeping hard, and covered in sweat, come, and slick.

For the sleep, Jason was grateful. Vale would need his rest. Still, he was slightly aroused again by the state of Vale's body. It was always part of the thrill of heat, how much mess came from their physical pleasure together. All the scents of it mixed together on their skin.

But there was no more time for him to think about that now. Jason quickly finished dressing and headed downstairs to call his parents.

With the heat well on its way, there was much to be done.

CHAPTER THREE

JASON

"PATER IS SICK." Ro poked glumly at his stewed apples and oatmeal. "Like Grandpater. Do all omegas get sick? Will he die?"

Jason had found Ro in his room crying when he'd finally gone looking for him that morning.

Ro had refused to tell him why he was so upset, and Jason had assumed he'd overheard something—Vale's cries or his own shout as he'd shot into the condom. Luckily, he hadn't knotted, or he'd have been stuck there for quite some time, possibly long enough for

Vale's first real swell to begin.

His son was eleven now but still naive in so many ways. His best friend Xan's son, Riki, was decidedly more worldly-wise than Ro, and he was almost six months younger. Ro still believed in winter-fox and, as far as Jason knew, was innocent to the ways of sex and heats. They'd coddled him too much. Kept him younger than his years.

Jason wished Vale were here for this conversation, but he wasn't, and given the state of him at the moment, he couldn't be. "At school, have they told you about the way babies are made?"

Ro frowned at his food and shook his head. "I've heard things, but none of it made a lot of sense."

"And Pater hasn't told you?"

It was lazy and selfish of him, but he'd always hoped Vale would handle this point of Ro's education sometime when Jason wasn't around. Vale had such a way with words and was a poet. Surely, he'd know how to make heat and fucking sound wonderful, beautiful, romantic, and not at all scary. Jason was a romantic at heart, too, but he was also pretty sure he had no idea how to explain it to Ro.

Vale would have been the better choice.

"Ro, do you know what an omega *is*?"

"Of course. Wolf-god made them to save humankind after the Great Death. You have to be an omega to be a pater," Ro said wretchedly. He hadn't eaten even a single bite of food, and his own pater would be here any moment to collect him. He brightened as a thought occurred. Maybe Pater could tell Ro about heat, sex, and knots? After all, Miner had explained it to Jason when he was young, and he'd done a good job of it.

"Yes," Jason agreed. "An omega is a man who can grow a baby inside."

Ro huffed. "I know that."

"An omega has a womb."

"I'm not dumb."

Jason kept his tone even. "And do you know how the baby gets inside the womb?"

"Wolf-god puts it there," Ro said with a miserable shrug. "Babies come from wolf-god."

"Ah, well, yes. But——"

"Darling!" Jason's pater rushed into the room, looking red-cheeked and shiny-eyed. If Jason didn't know better, he'd think his pater looked healthier and younger than he had in years. But he *did* know better, and when Pater immediately broke out into coughs that only heightened the color of his cheeks and the gloss of his eyes, Jason's heart ached.

"Grandpater," Ro moaned, abandoning the kitchen table to run to Miner. He grabbed Miner and buried his face against his shoulder. "Pater is sick!"

"Your pater isn't sick!" Miner exclaimed, looking at Jason in shock. "Why in wolf-god's name have you told him Vale's sick?"

"I didn't! I don't know why he——"

"Pater has been crying and yelling and begging," Ro said with a croak. "I heard him! He shouted, 'Please, please, please!'" Ro's imitation of Vale's desperation made Jason blush, and Miner blinked, clearly appalled. "Then he *screamed*!"

"Oh, baby," Miner said, clutching Ro tightly.

Ro's shoulders hitched, and Jason was surprised he didn't protest being called a baby. He was so very innocent about most things, but he was prideful.

Miner shot Jason a hard look. "Are you going to tell him? Or should I?"

Jason knew Vale would likely murder him for this, but he also knew he was short on time. The last rush of need in Vale had been too intense, and he had no doubt that true heat would start within the next few hours. He still needed to prepare food for the coming days and ready himself for the task of endless sex and knotting. Perhaps it made him a bad father, but he couldn't spend the time right now, and perhaps it made him an even *worse* father to feel relieved about that.

"You do it, please, Pater?"

Miner blinked in surprise but, after only a moment's hesitation, he nodded. "Come on, darling," he whispered in Ro's ear. "Come with Grandpater to his house. We'll have a wonderful few nights together. When Grandfather comes home tonight, we'll ring the bells for winter-fox together."

Ro stiffened again. He shook his head tightly. "I can't celebrate. Pater's sick! And it's all my fault!"

"Darling, no, it's not like that."

"Your pater isn't sick," Jason said, touching his son's hair again. "And even if he were, which he's not, it wouldn't be your fault."

Ro looked doubtful.

"Grandpater will explain everything," Jason went on. "What's happening is no one's fault. And your pater isn't sick."

"Your pater is perfectly fine," Miner said when Ro looked to him for verification of Jason's statement. It burned a little to know his son took Miner's word over his own, and for a moment, he understood Vale's feelings of jealousy.

Miner patted Ro's cheek. "I'll tell you everything you need to know about what's happening to your pater after you've had some tea and cookies at my house, all right?"

Ro wiped at his eyes with the back of his hand and whispered, "All right. But I have to get my things."

"Go pack a bag, darling, but be quick about it," Miner said tenderly, drying Ro's lashes with a handkerchief fished out of his pocket. "I promise everything is all right. We'll still celebrate the feast. So don't cry anymore, all right?"

Ro nodded and turned to leave the room, but he paused in the doorway. "You'd never lie to me, Grandpater?"

"I never would," Miner agreed.

"All right," Ro said with a firm nod that made Jason's heart ache. Did his son think *he* would lie? "I believe you."

Jason groaned as soon as they heard Ro's footsteps on the stairs up to his room.

"Thank you for taking him on such short notice."

"Of course! Having him with us is never a problem. I'm just sorry Vale is going through this again so soon." Miner touched Jason's cheeks with his fever-hot fingertips. "My sweet son. I know you're happy with him, but how I wish things had been different for you both."

"Pater…" Jason frowned as he heard a creak from the floorboards upstairs. Was Vale getting out of bed? He hoped not. Focusing on his pater again, he continued, "There's winter-fox to think of, please. Ro still believes."

"Don't worry, darling. Yule will stop by here on his way home from work and use his key to collect Ro's winter-fox presents. They're tucked away in Vale's study?"

"Yes. In the same cabinet where he hides Ro's birthday presents." Jason scrubbed at his face.

Miner lay his arm across Jason's shoulder, tugging him into a hug. "Darling, I know this is hard on you, too. All these fruitless heats."

Jason winced. He sometimes wished things *could* be different, but so long as he had Vale, he didn't mind the heats, fruitless or not.

Miner asked softly, "What does his doctor say?"

Jason's heart squeezed. "The doctors say it could be years of this." He turned away, opening cupboards, and checking the refrigerator. At least he'd been to the store earlier in the week to prepare for the feast they wouldn't be sharing as a family now. Feast of Winter's Heart was typically heavy on the sweets, but he'd laid in plenty of ingredients for some hearty meals, too. Vale never liked to gorge on just baked goods and candy, so Jason had what he needed to get them through the heat week.

"But interminable heat isn't a possibility, is it?" Miner asked cautiously, leaning his hip against the counter as Jason set about starting a meaty stew. Sometimes he could convince Vale to sip at it during the lulls in his heat. Wolf-god knew *he'd* need the sustenance after a few days of fucking.

"The doctors don't really know since they don't know what causes interminable heat." Jason frowned, cutting a carrot into rounds. "They *do* know of one way to make these surprise heats stop, though. At least for a while."

"Oh?"

"Pregnancy. And chestfeeding after the birth."

They met each other's eyes briefly and sighed.

"But since that isn't a possibility," Jason said, moving on to the parsley, "we'll just cope as best we can."

"It's unfortunate he's always had such an extremely poor reaction to heat suppressants."

"Urho says—"

"Dr. Chase! He's such a wonderful man."

"Yes, well…" Jason didn't disagree, but his pater's hero-worship of Dr. Chase was usually followed by suggestions that Vale have Urho perform the same surgery on him as he'd performed on Miner. Womb removal. But Jason had already discussed it with Urho, and that wasn't a solution for Vale's problem. His pater still had heats even after having his womb removed, and presumably, so would Vale. Scientists were learning that heats were determined by hormones released by multiple glands throughout the body and not simply by the presence of a womb. So, the surgery would be pointless. Vale would continue to endure surprise heats unless a new medicine could be found to alter his hormones.

But there was hope on the horizon! Which had been Jason's whole point in bringing up Urho, to begin with.

"Anyway, Urho says new trials are being done on a heat suppressant that can be implanted under the skin. It'll keep the drug steady and strong in an omega's body. No ups and downs, no need for a daily pill. It's a new delivery system, yes, but the really good news is that the suppressant is also a new, more reliable formula that works by regulating the hormones released by the omega's glands. It only works for about nine months, and then a heat must be had before they'll replace it, but it's hope."

"Ah, I've heard of this new drug," Miner said. "Much more cost-effective and safe. Not to mention the added layer of consent involved regarding pregnancy. That's always good for the omega. Though that's also what's keeping it hung up in the courts, too, I'd wager."

"The priests don't like to put obstacles in the way of conception," Jason agreed.

"No, they don't." Miner pressed his fingers to his lips, a habit he'd picked up since he'd quit smoking years ago. "Urho thinks it could work for Vale?"

"Yes. But he isn't sure when it will be freely available to the market."

"No, no, getting the approval of the priests in the government could be years coming." Miner moved his fingers from his mouth, almost as if he were smoking. "My friend Islay told me this new suppressant showed promise in omegas of all ages, though. Everyone from very young omegas to older contracted ones. He said the schools might insist on it for liability purposes, and some contracts may allow for the use of this suppressant even after a non-*Érosgápe* union with an alpha. If the alpha agrees, of course."

Jason said, "Most will. All alphas like happy omegas."

Miner shrugged. "Do they? We've both known of too many cases where omegas have been miserable, and their alpha hasn't cared a wit. To be fair, there are miserable alphas, too. But…" He waved his hand. "In any case, there's no dispute omegas have longed for more control over choosing to be bred, whether they're contracted or not."

"'To be bred,'" Jason muttered. "You make it sound like the law permits omegas to be treated like cattle."

"Well, we aren't carved up for meals," Miner conceded. "But we spend our entire lives being told in one way or another that our bodies are for our alpha's pleasure, and for growing and birthing their babies." Miner's lips tightened. "They have to brainwash us well to ensure we're willing to take the risk."

"Pater, you sound more and more like an omega rights extremist as you get older."

"Creeping death will do that to you," Miner said, his fingers twitching in the way that meant he was really craving a cigarette. "Don't tell me you aren't an omega rights activist yourself. You're the one who got arrested for it."

"That was because Xan…" Jason sighed. "Never mind. You're right. Of course, I support omega rights." Jason stopped preparing the stew and turned to his pater, pulse thumping horribly in his throat. "You almost slipped that news by me. Have the doctors decided then? Your illness is fatal?"

"No, they've said nothing of the kind," Miner said, waving a slim hand. "But I know I'm not all right, and your father can smell a change in me, and not a good one." He swallowed thickly. "Your father cries at night. I'm not a fool, son. Even if the doctors won't declare that I'm dying, I know." He swallowed hard. "*I* know what's happening."

"Pater…" Jason's heart ached. His pater was very sick, it was true. Ro wasn't wrong about that. Jason could smell the change himself, an acrid, horrible scent beneath his pater's standard, comforting smell. Jason felt dizzy just thinking of losing him.

"Jason, love, don't be like that." Miner smiled gently and came over to touch Jason's chin. "We were lucky to have so much time after Urho was able to help me. But the damage has been done. All those years of using the abortifacients.... My organs have never fully recovered from the toxins. Urho says I should count wolf-god's blessings that I've had as much time as I have."

"So, Urho *has* said it then." Jason stepped closer, eyes filling.

But his pater shook his head. "Don't, son. Not today. My heart won't bear it, and it isn't as though I'm dying right this moment." He smiled, and it was painful for them both. "You have a heat to attend to. There's no time for getting emotional now." Then with a bit of teasing in his voice, Miner went on, "Besides, I have to tell your child about the facts of life. *Really?* I'd have thought Vale would have done it himself by now."

"Don't pick on Vale," Jason warned, shaking a knife at his pater lightly. "He isn't you."

"You know I love Vale," Miner said, going to lean against the doorjamb. He glanced over his shoulder, obviously listening a moment for Ro. "Vale's a wonderful match for you and a good pater. He's a good man. There are so many things I admire in him." He looked around the messy kitchen and raised a brow. "Though housekeeping isn't one of them."

"Not that you have room to talk about that."

"No. But your father always keeps things neat. Besides, Vale's prickly with me ever since Ro came." Miner shrugged. "I think he's jealous. I'm sure *this* isn't going to help anything either."

"I'm ready," Ro said from the hallway, an overnight bag slung over his shoulder and his eyes still red from crying.

Jason strode to his son and pulled him close in a hug. "Enjoy the Feast of Winter's Heart with Grandpater and Grandfather, all right? I promise Pater is going to be fine."

Ro sniffled again. "I get it now. I know what's going on."

"What do you mean?"

"You said Pater isn't sick, so figured it out while I was packing," Ro said, his chin quivering and eyes filling with tears again.

"You did?" Jason asked as another wave of relief rushed over him. Perhaps Miner wouldn't need to explain it to Ro after all.

"You're breaking contract."

"What?" Jason gasped. "That's…not possible."

"Literally impossible," Miner added, coming to put his hand on Ro's head. "They're *Érosgápe*. They can't break contract. They can't *stop loving* each other."

"Keifer told me when his parents got separate houses, his pater cried and wailed for a week beforehand," Ro said. "Just like Pater was crying. I know what I heard."

"Oh, wolf-god, bless this child," Miner murmured. "Keifer's parents weren't *Érosgápe*, were they? Of course, not. As for the rest, well, I'll take care of it," he said to Jason over Ro's dark head. "Let's go, darling. I'll explain everything when you're settled in at home with me."

"I love your pater more than life," Jason whispered in Ro's ear as he hugged him. He pulled back to look his son in the eye as he went on, "And he loves me, too. We both love *you*. Never doubt it. Everything here is fine. No one is moving houses. So, promise me you'll enjoy the Feast of Winter's Heart with your grandparents. It might be your last year celebrating. You're growing so fast. Winter-fox may mistake you for a teenager next year."

Ro frowned and studied Jason's eyes, but he said nothing. He kissed Jason's cheek solemnly and then walked with Miner from the house.

Jason followed as far as the front porch. When Ro took off running across the muddy yard toward the waiting Sabel car, Jason grabbed his pater in a hug. "Thank you," he whispered again. "I love you so much."

"I love you, too. Take care of Vale," Miner said with a sad smile. "I wish things could be different. I understand the heartbreak of fruitless heats all too well."

"I know you do, Pater." Jason kissed his pater's cheek.

Jason hadn't lied to Vale when he'd said the lack of children didn't bother him. Vale was his life, and all that mattered was his safety and joy. Fruitless heats were still ecstatic, and he didn't regret any knot he shared with Vale, child or no child.

Miner climbed into the car with Ro, and the driver whisked them both away. It was only once the car had turned a corner and was no longer visible that Jason went back into the house. Shutting the door, he shivered to hear Vale cry out from the bedroom above.

Every cell in his body answered with a keen explosion of sensation and a matching desperation of his own. Jason took the stairs two at a time to get to his *Erosgápe*.

The heat had begun.

CHAPTER FOUR

RO

IF THERE WAS one thing Viro Sabel truly hated, it was lies.

Ro prided himself on being an honest boy. More honest than any of his friends. Never once had he told an untruth. He'd withheld information, obviously, and he'd phrased his words very carefully so that he didn't *have* to lie—which was very hard because he wasn't as smart as some of his friends—but he'd never just up and bald-faced lied about anything. In return, Ro expected absolute honesty from all the important people in his life.

But Ro was very worried his parents were lying to him now. Or his father was anyway. He'd heard Pater's cries and groans for himself, and he knew those couldn't come from anything good or even from something that wasn't actually very, *very* bad.

One of the only times Ro had made similar noises was when he'd been horribly sick with a stomach virus and kept throwing up. In between puking, he'd cried and sobbed and screamed in frustration. The other time had been when he'd fallen while climbing over the backyard fence and skinned his knee, he'd made a similar gasping-hurt sound just as he'd hit the ground. What could possibly make his pater sound like *that* for almost an hour?

But while his father might lie to him—disappointing, but true—Grandpater would not. He had vowed he would *never*.

And yet…and yet…

He *had* to be lying now, right?

"The alpha puts his penis in the omega's

butt?" Ro wrinkled his nose as he repeated his grandpater's words to make sure he understood. "Because the omega hurts if he doesn't? That doesn't make sense."

"During heat, the omega's internal glands are swollen with slick and require the pressure of the alpha's penis to release it. Also, during heat, the omega requires his alpha's knot to push against his inner glands, *and* he needs to scent his alpha's pheromones to fully relieve the pain. It's like a very scented massage in a way."

Grandpater sat on the sofa in his special conservatory, a room similar in function, if not in atmosphere, to Ro's pater's study. Ro sat beside him, listening intently. None of this was what he'd ever expected to hear.

"His knot?" Ro blinked. "*What* knot?"

"Ah, well, I see they haven't explained anything at all, have they?"

"No?"

"During heat, and after penetration, the base of an alpha's penis will swell once climax is achieved." Grandpater made a fist, Ro assumed, to demonstrate the size of this knot. "Climax is the pinnacle of pleasure during the joining of bodies." He frowned, seeming a little flustered. "And, ah, you can join bodies any time you want, but the knot only happens during heat."

Ro was beginning to piece it together, but it was all quite disturbing.

Grandpater wrapped his hand around the base of his fist. "The knot locks the alpha into the omega's body, tight inside his anus until enough time has passed."

Ro pushed his plate of half-eaten cookies across the coffee table until it sat next to the pot of tea. "How much time?"

"It depends." Grandpater shrugged. "Sometimes ten minutes, sometimes an hour."

"But why?"

"To give his semen time to fertilize the egg in the omega's womb."

"But *why?*" Ro wanted to pound the

coffee table. But he knew Grandpater would say that wasn't dignified behavior and that he was getting too old for those kinds of theatrics.

Besides, Grandpater looked so tired now Ro didn't want to upset him. He suspected this conversation, and Ro's disbelieving questions, were already upsetting him more than enough.

"It's how wolf-god decided to save us from extinction after the Great Death." Grandpater looked a little confused himself, like he either didn't fully understand what he was claiming happened between alphas and omegas, or he hadn't expected it to be so hard to explain.

"But *why*?" Ro asked again, trying to stay calm. Even he could hear the hint of hysteria in his voice. "We *poop* out of our butts. And…and…wouldn't it hurt to put something big in there?"

He'd seen his father's penis, and it was enormous. Now Grandpater was sitting here calmly claiming that at certain times that penis would grow even bigger and harder—like how Ro's penis grew when he rubbed it against his mattress in his sleep at night—and that his father would push that big thing into his pater's butthole.

Grandpater had *even* said the alpha's penis *ached* to be inside the omega's butt, like it had a mind of its own or something horrible like that. But Ro really couldn't imagine how that could be true. He would never *ache* to put his cock in a butt, would he? How absurd. Grandpater had to be lying.

And yet…

Grandpater sure was sticking to his story, because he went on explaining, "Well, omegas' anuses and passages aren't made like alpha or beta anuses and colons are. That's how we can tell them apart at birth, remember?"

"Yes, like Riki," Ro said, mentioning his omega family friend and pseudo-cousin. "We already know he's an omega, but we have to wait to see that I'm an alpha."

"Exactly. We didn't need to wait for him to present like with you. We knew at his birth."

Ro grew thoughtful again. "What's different about them? Their butts, I mean."

"Oh, lots of things," Grandpater said and then started to cough. He couldn't seem to stop for a long time and eventually had to get his handkerchief from his cardigan's pocket and cough into it. When he stopped, he wiped at his mouth, grimaced at the handkerchief, and then quickly folded it and tucked it back into his pocket. He didn't continue talking, looking a little gray.

"Are you all right, Grandpater?"

Grandpater patted Ro's head and reached to fill their empty cups with Ro's favorite flavor of tea: chocolate-mint. "Don't worry about me. Do you understand everything I've been telling you?"

Ro thought for a long time, picking up a cookie, but feeling too conflicted to take a bite, he sat it back down on the plate. "You said during heat Father thrusts into Pater's butt with his penis because it makes Pater hurt less? But if that's true, why was Pater crying and groaning and yelling like that?"

Grandpater's ears turned quite red as he sipped his own cup of tea and directed his gaze out the wide, conservatory window out onto the back gardens that hired beta servants kept so well-planted and neat. "Have you ever been tickled?"

Ro shuddered. "Yes. I hate it."

"So do I. Perhaps this isn't a good analogy then, but it's the best one I've got right now. I think I did a better job when I told your father about all of this when he was young. I'm finding the right words are harder to come by than I expected." Grandpater sipped his tea again and then went on, "When you're tickled, doesn't some part of it almost feel good?"

Ro tried to remember the last time he'd been tickled, and as he did, he ran his fingers over his arm lightly, feeling the pleasant tingle over his skin. Goosebumps rose, and he shivered. "Some soft touches feel good," he agreed. "But tickling is *bad*. I hate it."

"Yes. Well, when the alpha puts his penis in the omega, the feeling for them both is *very* good, and then the good feeling grows and grows and *grows* until it's so intense the omega can't help but gasp and moan because it feels *so* good, you see."

Ro brushed his arm slowly again until he couldn't help but press harder, rubbing away the tingle.

Grandpater went on, "But it's *not* like tickling because it doesn't ever turn into something bad. It just gets to be so good that you can't stop from moaning and crying out."

He looked mortified as he explained, and it suddenly occurred to Ro, and he didn't know why it hadn't before, that Grandpater and Grandfather must have done this penis-in-butthole-during-heat thing at least once to have had Father. And Grandpater had *liked* it. He'd liked it so much he'd cried out and groaned and made the pain-but-not-pain noises. So weird.

Ro chewed on the inside of his cheek. It still felt like it had to be a lie, and yet it obviously wasn't.

"Father does that to Pater? And Pater likes it so much he cries?"

"With joy, yes. With pleasure and good feelings," Grandpater said, patting Ro's hand where it rested on the table next to his teacup. "It sounds strange now, but when you're older, and you've presented—or not—"

"I'll present!"

"—then you'll feel this tug for yourself, especially if you meet your *Érosgápe*. You won't be able to stop yourself from wanting to be inside him. You'll scent him and know immediately that he's yours. It will be the most beautiful and dangerous moment of your life because there are rules about how an alpha must treat an omega, even when under the sway of their hormones and the *Érosgápe* instinct. But I'll let your parents explain the rest to you," Grandpater said, and he sounded even more tired. "I'm afraid I haven't been very clear, and I've muddled the entire thing."

"No, I understand," Ro said, though he didn't entirely. "I just don't believe I'll ever want to do that with any omega. Definitely not with Riki."

He and Riki had already promised each other that if he *did* present as an alpha—and he would!—they'd contract with each other when they grew up.

Well, if they never met their *Érosgápe* mate, that is.

And now that he knew what to expect if he ever did meet his *Érosgápe*? He thought he'd rather have Riki instead. Then he'd never have to put his penis in any omega's butt. Riki wouldn't want him to do that either, surely.

Though Riki might want him to do it

if…

"Grandpater, omegas don't go into heat if they don't meet their *Érosgápe*, right?"

"What? Oh, darling, yes. It's biological. All omegas endure heat."

"All of them?" Ro felt a creeping horror down his spine.

"Yes, of course."

Suddenly, Ro realized that he'd already known the truth underneath his hope. After all, many of his friends' parents were not *Érosgápe*, and they'd made children.

"Any alpha can help them through it. There are condoms—a sheath to cover the penis and catch the semen—to prevent pregnancy. Many young omegas take suppressant pills to keep the heat at bay until they are ready to experience it with an alpha they like, or ideally with their *Érosgápe*."

"Why doesn't Pater take the heat suppressant pills?"

"They're only for young omegas," Grandpater said with a frown. "They don't work as well with older men. There can be bad side effects. But, darling, I think you should save the rest of your questions for your parents, don't you? They'll be able to explain it all much better than I can."

Ro thought Grandpater had explained it well enough for him to know he wanted exactly *nothing* to do with any of it. For the first time ever, he wasn't at all excited by the idea of growing up and presenting. His body betraying him? Making him want to put such a sensitive part of himself into a butthole? It just seemed horrible.

He wondered if Riki knew.

Ro half-heartedly finished off his cookies while Grandpater leaned back on the sofa and rested. After a while, Grandpater's head lolled, and his mouth dropped open. Ro's heart twisted in his chest, watching his grandpater's eyes move lightly beneath his silky eyelids as he slept.

Pater might not be sick, but Grandpater definitely was. Everyone knew it, and no one denied it. He studied his grandpater's face, noting how the wrinkles smoothed out in his sleep, making him look younger.

After a few minutes, Ro carefully collected the dishes and carried them toward the kitchen. Unlike in his own home, where Father did all the cleaning, he knew he was expected to deal with his own mess here.

After washing the dishes and putting them away, he headed toward his second favorite place in the house: his father's old room.

There he flopped onto the bed, staring up at the ceiling and thinking hard. Several minutes passed before he rolled onto his side and picked up the telephone extension his grandparents had installed sometime after his father had moved out. Every time his father came into the room now, he remarked on it. "What's the use of a telephone in here now? I'm gone."

But Grandfather was like that. He enjoyed using his money to buy newly developed or re-developed technology. And when he'd heard that other men had put phone extensions in every bedroom, he'd followed suit, which worked out well for Ro whenever he stayed over.

Which he did a lot.

And now he knew that was because of this…this wolf-god forsaken *heat* thing.

Whenever he slept over, Ro liked to call Riki, and they'd stay up into the night, laughing and making up games or stories. Riki didn't have a phone in his room, though. He had to take the calls in his father's library. The first few times, Ro had been worried that Riki wouldn't be allowed to stay up talking. But Riki had younger siblings, and his parents left him to himself most of the time now. Sometimes they even forgot to keep track of him or make sure he went to bed at all. They just assumed, as the oldest, he was where he was supposed to be, doing what he was supposed to do, and usually, he was. Which meant Riki could take advantage of that trust sometimes to break the rules. Like staying up until after midnight talking with Ro by telephone.

But Ro didn't want to talk by phone today. He had too much to get off his chest.

"Hello. Is Riki there?" he said into the receiver and then waited for the beta servant who'd answered to find his friend.

At least Riki was in the city for the holidays. Some years, the Heelies family stayed the full winter up in Virona—the town Ro was named for, having been born there himself—and, during those months, Ro was too lonely. He had friends at school, of course, but none of them understood him like Riki.

"Viro?" Riki's calm voice slipped over the line. Riki was the only person to call Ro by that name. Everyone else just called him Ro, even his teachers at school. "Hi!"

"I'm at my grandparents' house. Wanna come over?"

"Really?"

There were some shouts and crashes in the background and the sound of an adult scolding one of the other children, but Ro wasn't sure who was in trouble. Probably Levi. Maybe Bek. Or possibly even Sam. Nor could Ro rule out all of them acting as a chaotic team. He didn't know why the Heelies kids were so wild, but they sure were. Unless Riki's pater, Caleb, was around, *then* everyone acted like little angels. But Ro didn't get that either, because while Caleb was strict and expected good behavior, he never even raised his voice.

"Absolutely. I'll be right there."

Bam, scream.

"Sorry. Things are loud here," Riki went on. "Lots of—" *crash, shout* "—stuff going on."

"Meet me on the roof."

"Got it."

The call disconnected, and Ro stood up to investigate what clothes were in his father's old closet. Ro had some warm things he kept here for snowy days when he'd come over to play and sled down the big back hill. And while it was chilly outside now, it wasn't exactly frigid. The ground was more damp than frozen. It would make for a yucky Feast of Winter's Heart if the snows didn't come.

Deep in the closet, he found a heavy sweater, leftover from when his father was young, and pulled it on over his clothes. He grabbed some mittens from the drawer next to his father's old desk. Looking in the mirror, he took in his wide blue eyes, his pale skin, and his fringe of dark hair. He was tall for his age, but something about his face looked a little breakable. He knew he was strong, though, and would grow stronger every day.

Nodding at his reflection, he added a knit cap and opened the bedroom window.

The roof outside of his father's bedroom was flat and offered a clear view of the street, the city, and the sky. A tree next to the house stretched up, etching the sky with black lines of limbs. There was a trellis of roses that came up the side of the house, too. Earlier in the year when he'd just turned eleven, and Riki was still ten, Riki had tried to climb up the trellis to the roof, fallen, and broken his wrist.

Pater had been furious. He considered the roof dangerous for kids Riki and Ro's age. But Father had always said he'd sat out on the roof himself most of his life, and Xan had climbed the trellis plenty of times, so they'd be fine to do the same.

But it'd just been bad luck that Riki had fallen.

Riki's parents hadn't been nearly so upset, even though their son had been the one to get hurt. Urho, the doctor who always lived with Riki's family, had set Riki's bones and said it would be at least three months before he climbed up anything again.

But Riki's parents didn't forbid him from climbing, not like Pater had tried to forbid Ro. Which seemed completely unfair since Ro hadn't even been the one to fall or climb at all. He'd never had a chance!

It'd taken a lot of wheedling for Father to convince Pater to allow for Ro to go out on the roof again. Ro had been made to promise to always be careful. But, of course, he would be careful! He didn't want to get hurt, and he was no dummy!

After that, though, Grandpater started keeping a very sturdy ladder up against the side of the house next to Father's old bedroom for them to use. Ro was glad no one had insisted Riki come in through the front door like any other friend. It was more exciting that he was allowed to climb in through the window like a bandit or a thief, and Ro's heart still beat fast when he thought about it that way.

Ro kept the rooftop spot a secret from his other friends. It was special, just for the two of them. Because *Riki* was special.

Ro's heart tugged a certain weird sort of way whenever he looked at Riki. It left him a little dizzy. That was why they'd agreed to contract when they were older if they didn't find their *Érosgápes*.

But now, knowing about omegas and heat and penises-going-in-butts, Ro wasn't sure he wanted to contract with *any* omega, ever.

He really wanted to know what Riki knew about it all, and what he thought about this outrageous heat business. Even though Riki was an omega and younger, he always had really good ideas.

And Riki had never lied to Ro. At least not so far as Ro knew.

Out on the roof, he stared up at the winter-bright atmosphere. The sky was clear, which meant no snow for the first night of the bells. There would still be lights, candles, and decorations, and the bells would still ring, and the sound would rise in the streets, but without snow, it'd all feel a little less magical.

As it should, now that he knew the truth.

Ro studied the Feast of Winter's Heart decorations draped on some of the other nearby houses—well, mansions—lining his grandparents' street. Silver, gold, and glittery bobbles hung everywhere. The decorations were all beautiful, but all lies. There was no winter-fox, no magic brother of wolf-god delivering presents and demanding sweets, and while Ro had known before he'd asked his pater—he really had!—he was a little sad about it anyway.

Even if the bells rang and the priests chanted and the decorations shone, it wouldn't be the same. Everything was different now.

Growing up and learning new truths about life didn't seem nearly so great all of a sudden. No winter-fox. No magic at all. Unless you counted *Érosgápe*—and heats and knots, and the weird uncontrollable urge to put penises in butts.

All of that was a kind of magic, wasn't it? Wolf-god's weird, gross magic that Ro didn't ever want any part of.

Which made him feel guilty.

Because wolf-god loved him and had designed all of that gross stuff to save men from extinction.

Grandpater said so.

The ladder rattled at the side of the house, and Ro's heart leapt.

Soon Riki's dark head popped up over the edge of the roofline. A red hat covered his curly hair, and an even redder cape swathed his slim form. He was smiling, of course—he always was—and he hauled himself up over the edge with a pleasant-sounding grunt. Somehow everything Riki did was elegant. Even climbing a ladder and grunting. Even crying, as Ro well remembered from when he'd broken his arm.

Riki was probably the most beautiful boy Ro had ever seen. That was another reason he'd made Riki promise to contract with him if they didn't find an *Érosgápe*, because Ro wanted to have that beauty as his own. He knew once he presented, he'd be proud to have such a beautiful omega by his side. *His. All his.*

"Thanks for asking me over," Riki said, crawling over the roof tiles to sit beside Ro. "My brothers are all being…" He waved his hands around. "Ugh. At least Pater took the baby with him. He cries so much." Riki pulled his red cape around his shoulders and sighed. "Just between you and me, I really hope Pater is done with babies."

Ro nodded. The new baby was boring, all of Riki's brothers were really. But the second youngest, Sam, was somewhat interesting to Ro. Lots of people had whispered about him when he was first born, but Ro wasn't sure why. Maybe it was because Sam's skin was so dark? In that way, he *did* look very different from the rest of the Heelies children. But wolf-god was mysterious, Grandpater had said when Ro had asked about it. Sam was a cute kid, so it didn't really matter.

"Speaking of babies," Ro said, sitting up tall. "I know something you don't know." He was proud of this likely fact. It was rare for Riki not to know more than him. He was even ahead of Ro at school, despite being technically younger.

"Oh yeah?" Riki said, sitting straight. "What's that?"

"I know how babies get made."

"Wolf-god makes them," Riki said with a narrow gaze.

"No, fathers and paters make them. With their *bodies*."

Riki rolled his eyes. "Oh. Right. Well, everyone knows that."

Ro drew back. "No, they don't!"

"Maybe *you* didn't know, but everyone else knows."

"That's not true!" Ro couldn't be the only one who didn't know. That would be way too embarrassing. And Riki was almost six months younger than him! He was bluffing. He had to be. "Explain it then!

How does it work?!"

Riki's blue eyes went a little serious, and he shifted uncomfortably. "What if *you* don't know? I'm not supposed to tell other kids about it. Urho said it's every family's right to—"

"I know about the alpha's penis going in the omega's butt," Ro announced, chin up.

"Oh," Riki said, and then he giggled, his eyes going down to the roof slates. His cheeks grew red, and it wasn't from the cold. "Yes. That's part of it."

"And heat."

"Yes, heat," Riki said, and he squirmed a little. Somehow still elegantly, though, like he was a fairy or a sprite.

"What do you think of it?"

"Of heat?"

"Of all of it."

Riki went very still and then whispered, "It's scary. Heat, I mean. That's why an omega needs a strong alpha to protect him. That's what pater says."

"Why is it scary?"

"I don't know. It just is." Riki lifted the edge of his cape and covered his face. "Pater told me it just *happens*, and you can't stop it. Why wouldn't that be scary?"

"I think it sounds gross. Why would I want to put my—" Ro gestured at his crotch "—in your—" he wrinkled his nose. "You poop from there."

Riki didn't say anything more, just picking at the edge of his cape, and Ro felt like he'd said something wrong, but he didn't know why. "Hmm," Riki finally said quietly. "Well, that's how it happens. So…" He shrugged.

Ro stared at him, admiring the way his cheeks grew pinker with the cold.

"By the way, why are you over here?" Riki asked, tilting his head. "The bells start tonight. Shouldn't you be with your—" he broke off and his eyes grew knowing. "Oh. Your pater. Another heat?"

Ro wondered why Riki sounded so

empathetic, but he simply said. "Yeah. Grandpater said Pater went into heat early, so I have to be here for the celebrations and the Feast of Winter's Heart."

"Winter-fox will find you. Don't worry," Riki said reassuringly.

Ro stared at his friend. Did Riki also know about winter-fox? He'd known about heat and sex and babies, so Ro bet he *did* know. So embarrassing to think that Riki knew so much more than he did about so many things. He wondered what Riki would think of Ro pretending to believe in winter-fox when he didn't really? Had Riki been doing the same?

Finally, Ro asked, "If you knew something that the grownups didn't want you to know yet, would you tell them you knew it?"

Riki looked up sharply. "Your parents don't want you to know about how babies are made yet?"

"No, it's something else." Ro cleared his throat and said even more carefully, "Say you're supposed to believe in something that's not true, but your parents want you to believe it because it's fun for them? And if you *don't* believe it, then everyone misses out on certain things—fun things, like presents."

Riki's eyebrow popped up. "Is this about winter-fox?"

"No! I didn't say anything about winter-fox!" If Riki didn't know yet, he shouldn't spoil it for him at the last minute. But it was really hard to decide if he was doing the right thing by not telling Grandpater and Grandfather he knew the truth, even if Pater had encouraged him to stay quiet.

"I think it *is* about winter-fox," Riki said, shoving one of his dark curls behind his ear.

"Do *you* know about winter-fox?"

Riki shrugged.

Ro sighed and crossed his arms over his chest, feeling every bit five months older. *Finally.* "You have to say one way or another, or I can't tell you anything else."

Riki's blue eyes twinkled. "Ro, I think

we *both* know about winter-fox. That seems pretty obvious to me. Isn't it to you?"

"So you know winter-fox isn't…you know. And that it's really…our…" He stared at Riki with wide eyes.

"Parents?"

He let loose with a big sigh, half disappointment, and half relief. He was tired of Riki always knowing more than him, but he really did want to talk this over. "Oh, you do know."

"Of course." Riki sighed. "I told my parents last year, and they said I needed to pretend for a few more seasons so the little ones don't catch on. What did your parents say?"

Ro couldn't believe how lightly adults seemed to take the truth sometimes. "Pater wants me to pretend, too. For Father's sake, and for my grandparents' sake." Ro took a slow breath. "You don't think it's a lie? To pretend?"

"If it is, there's really no victim, right? It

doesn't hurt anyone."

"But what about wolf-god? It goes against the spirit of the holiday. It goes against the spirit of the Holy Book of Wolf."

"Wolf-god has more to worry about than if kids pretend to believe in winter-fox or not," Riki said.

"But it's against the teachings."

"If your pater said it was all right, then it's all right."

They sat in silence as Ro considered whether he agreed with that or not. In the end, he still didn't know. But he was tired of sitting on the cold roof while Riki stared up at the sky and said nothing.

"Do you wanna play a game?" Ro finally asked after the weird silence had drawn out way too long.

Riki nodded but stayed quiet.

"Inside or outside?"

"Inside," Riki said, his tone a little distant. "It's cold out here."

"Board game or pretend game?"

"Board game."

Ro nodded and turned back to the window he'd left open. "I bet you win again. You always win. It's not fair. I'm older than you and an alpha."

"You don't know that. You're not an alpha *for sure*," Riki said, following Ro into the house.

"I'll present!" Ro exclaimed again, shutting the window behind them and locking it for good measure. "I'll present, I promise, and if we don't find our *Érosgápe*—" at this, he sneered lightly because he really hoped he *didn't*, now that he knew "—you'll be my omega." A light feeling warmed his chest at the thought.

Riki frowned. "If it turns out you're a beta, we've promised for nothing."

Ro grinned and plucked the red beanie off Riki's head of black curls. "I'm an alpha. I know it."

Riki chewed on his lip. "*If* you are, and *if* I still promise—"

"You already promised! You can't take it back now!"

Riki crossed his arms over his chest. "Then do you promise to handle my heats?"

"Ew."

"Viro," he said seriously. "I can't swear if you won't do it."

"You *already* swore, and I know you, Riki, you're no liar. But all right. Fine. I promise to handle your heats." Ro shuddered. "So gross."

Riki looked momentarily troubled, but then he nodded. "All right. We both promise."

"Why do you sound sad about it?" Ro asked, a little annoyed at Riki's reluctance.

"I'm not sad."

"You are."

"I'm not!"

"Don't lie!"

"It's just…" Riki flushed. "It's not supposed to be gross, Viro. I don't want it to be gross."

"It *is* gross. You can't help that."

Riki flinched. "Viro—"

"Come on, let's play. I'm sorry I brought it up."

Riki followed Ro from the room, and they headed down to his grandfather's study to where the board games were kept in a cabinet behind his desk. They'd play in there until Grandpater woke and sent Riki home or until Grandfather came home to start dinner. Or until the dusk dropped down, and the time came to stand on the stoop and ring the bells as a family. Riki would want to be home for that.

Later, as Riki rolled the dice and moved his piece forward on the board, he asked, "Do you really promise, Viro?"

"Of course."

"Even if it's gross?" Riki said, his finely drawn eyebrows furrowing.

"Pfft. I'll be an alpha. No, I *am* an alpha." He drew himself up again, trying to look bigger than he was. "That means I'll take care of my omega."

"All right," Riki agreed. "I trust you."

Pride bloomed in him like a winter rose. Riki was right to trust him. So long as no *Érosgápe* interfered, he'd take care of Riki forever, even through a heat. He'd promised.

He rolled the dice and crowed as he moved his piece to victory.

CHAPTER FIVE
YULE

YULE TUCKED THE last of the boxes into the trunk of his car.

As he'd carried Ro's presents from his son's house—ignoring the sounds from upstairs indicating the pleasure of intense heat—he'd noted the careful wrapping and the care taken with each bow. Vale wasn't much of a housekeeper, but when it came to presents, he was quite meticulous, expressing his affection with each corner tucked neatly and a flamboyantly written note attached.

Yule checked the tree he'd strapped atop the car, having stopped at a Winter's Heart

Fair on his way over. He then double-checked the boxes of fresh garlands and ribbons in the back seat, too. It'd been so many years since he and Miner had the joy of putting out the decorations, doing a special tree, and leaving out presents. They hadn't celebrated the feast in their own home since Jason was a child. It was an unexpected pleasure to get to indulge in the magic of the season again for the sake of his one and only grandson.

Yule pulled away from the decidedly middle-class house his son and his son's omega chose to live in. It was a lovely little home, even if it was haphazardly cared for inside, but Yule didn't understand why Jason chose it over moving into a residence more befitting of their net worth and anticipated inheritance. Jason said it was due to Vale's attachment to his family home, but surely the man would become equally attached to a mansion on the proper side of town? Some things Yule would never understand.

But as his own pater had often said, wolf-god alone knew why young people did even half the things they chose to do. Indeed, Yule's pater had often made such remarks when he and Miner were first contracted, the sentiment always muttered in a disapproving voice with a dark glare at Miner. Ah, yes, Yule's pater had been quite controlling, and Miner had been miserable over the emotional manipulations and outright machinations.

Because of that history, Yule and Miner had tried to stay out of Jason and Vale's way.

Eventually. Once the contract was set.

Still, Yule hadn't been surprised to get Miner's message that their grandson, Ro, would be staying with them for the Feast of Winter's Heart due to yet another of Vale's sudden heats. Vale had been having problems with his heats and fertility for most of his adult life. It was yet another reason why Yule still secretly stood by his initial position that Jason should have spurned the *Érosgápe* connection—as difficult as it would have been—and taken on a surrogate omega instead.

But that had never been a popular opinion in his small family. Miner had nearly broken Yule's heart with his vehement disagreement, and Jason wouldn't even consider it right from the start. Jason had known his own mind, determined to be with his mate from the moment he'd seen Vale.

Ah, yes, Yule was proud of his stubborn son. Still, things might have been easier had a different choice been made. Even though Jason would never have been as happy with another omega, Yule couldn't help but think if Jason had taken his advice, he'd at least have had more options. *And* more children.

At least he wouldn't be tied to the unpredictable cycles of an omega who could never give him more children. They'd all known of his defects from the start.

Where's your charity? Your compassion? Miner's chiding voice echoed in his head.

Yule winced lightly. Miner had always

possessed more of both those virtues than he ever had.

But Miner was right, of course. Vale couldn't help who he was or who he'd been, nor could he change his past or his fate. Wolf-god alone knew what was best, and he'd made Vale and Jason a pair, and he'd helped them find each other.

Yule and Miner could only support Jason and his family through whatever may come.

The Sabel-Hoff house wasn't far away. Shortly he pulled into his driveway and parked outside his beautiful home: a testament to his hard work and the work of those who came before him. Even though he'd lived in the house for nearly forty years, he still admired the sharp lines of the stone façade and the sheer size of the exterior. Inside, the house was homier—the way Miner preferred—but the outside spoke of wealth and power. Yule liked that. It made him feel strong and proud like he could protect Miner—and Jason—from anything.

Never mind that he'd been utterly una-ble to protect either of them when it'd truly mattered the most.

Shaking off that morbid thought, Yule climbed out, opened the back door, and loaded up his arms with several boxes of decorations. As he headed toward the house, the front door burst open, and dark-haired Ro darted out.

"Grandfather!" he called. "Let me help you!"

Glad the winter-fox gifts were safely hidden in the trunk, Yule handed off some of his burden to his grandson, who shouldered them with a grave seriousness—a sweet imitation of adulthood—that almost made Yule laugh.

"Are you excited for the bells tonight?" Yule asked as they carried the decorations up the front stairs to the still-open front door. Oh well, he'd scold the boy another day. Or never.

Ro shrugged. "I suppose."

"After winter-fox stops coming, once all a family's children have grown up," Yule said, dropping the boxes in the hallway. "The bells become the best part."

"Because there isn't a feast anymore? Or presents?"

"Exactly so." He put the box down in the front hall and ruffled Ro's hair. "But it's good to have a little one in the house now. Winter-fox will come again!"

Ro smiled, but something sad flickered behind his eyes. Yule supposed he must be disappointed to be away from his parents. They'd just have to make this year even more special for him.

"Guess what?"

"What?"

"I've taken the next few days off so we can decorate and bake and get all the sweets ready for the feast. Where's Grandpater?" Yule asked. He looked around for Miner and was relieved to see him emerge from his conservatory, looking no sicker than usual.

His beloved had endured so much in life. It hardly seemed fair that there was more pain ahead. For both of them. Yule again shook the thought from his mind. In the meantime, they had their grandson with them, a feast to celebrate, and more joy to be had. The pain would come in due time.

Miner smelled sweet like he'd been sleeping, and, as he drew close, he gave Yule a kiss on the cheek. "You bought a tree?"

"Of course! And more decorations than I know what to do with!" Yule tugged Miner against his side and sniffed at his hair, his heart aching with love as he grinned. "We'll have a grand old time, won't we, Ro?"

And again, Ro's eyes grew a little dimmer, but he simply scuffed his foot against the floor in the wide entryway, frowning at the boxes of decorations. "Yes."

Miner tilted his head at Yule, indicating that he should handle Ro's worries.

"You miss your parents?" Yule asked, pulling Ro close against his side, too, bringing him into a group hug. He patted Ro's back reassuringly. "I'm sure they miss you, too, but they'd want you to have a good time with us."

Ro smiled at him. "I know. Pater wanted you both to enjoy this year a lot."

"He did?"

"Yes, he said so. Before the heat started. He wanted you and Grandpater to have fun, like a gift." Ro looked him in the eye, his gaze determined instead of sad. "What about the tree, Grandfather? Should we bring it in now?"

Meeting Miner's smile with his own, Yule agreed. "Of course! Let's get it down from the car and take it into the den by the fireplace. We'll decorate it before dinner."

"Can I help cook?" Ro asked. "Father's been trying to teach me at home. He says you're the best cook in the world."

"Well, I don't know about that," Yule said, chuffed all the same. "I'm sure you can help, though. I was thinking pasta?"

Ro's eyes brightened again, and he nodded eagerly. "With meat sauce?"

"I think I have some beef, so certainly."

"Let's get the tree, Grandfather, and get started. I'm hungry."

Yule chuckled and brushed his fingers through Ro's soft, dark hair. He couldn't believe how tall the boy was getting. Up to his shoulder now. He opened the front door again and indicated that Ro should head on out. "After you."

Ro dashed into the cold afternoon sunlight. Yule's heart sang.

"I'll go listen to music while you two deal with that," Miner said, sounding tired despite smelling of recent sleep. "Don't forget the bells begin just after sunset. We'll want to be out front in plenty of time." Miner hesitated and then went on, "I have a lot to tell you, but…later."

Yule kissed Miner's lips again, his heart quickening with its usual joy to be so close to the most beautiful, perfect man he'd ever

known. Infuriating though he'd often been when he was younger. "I missed you a lot today."

Miner's lips twitched. "You say that every day."

"It's true every—"

"Grandfather!" Ro called from outside.

"Go on." Miner pushed Yule toward the door, but before joining Ro out in the cold air, Yule paused to watch Miner's long form saunter down the hallway. The way his body moved always made Yule want to grab and kiss him again.

"Grandfather!"

No time for that though.

Yule joined Ro by the car, and together they untied the tree and worked it down from the top of the car.

Several happy hours later, he and Ro had decorated its branches, twisted tinsel around the banisters, and cooked a meal that had left Miner humming with each bite. Yule's heart felt softer and warmer with each passing minute, as though his own youthful faith in winter-fox was pushing to the surface to make everything magical again.

As for his time with Ro, it was a delight. The boy was full of funny stories and interesting (though often somewhat wrong) facts, and many strong opinions. Sipping his wine and looking at Miner and Ro over their now empty dishes, he let the warm glow of contentment settle in his bones.

After dinner, they headed out to the front porch together, all of them eager for the bells to begin. Miner bundled up carefully, but Yule made sure he wore an extra scarf to protect his neck, and as they waited, Yule adjusted the warm, knit cap on Miner's head.

Miner rolled his eyes but indulged him, and then Yule turned to Ro and adjusted his hat as well. After quickly kissing Miner's cheek, he passed out the bells—two sets of sleigh bells on a stick and one traditional brass bell with a clapper. He took hold of Ro's free hand, surprised the boy still let him hold it at his age, but pleased that he did. They all held their bells at the ready.

Their neighbors stood on their front porches, too, across the street and to either side. The road running in front of their houses was already empty of cars in anticipation of the parade. Soon priests from the Holy Church of Wolf would stream into the streets with their holy bells jangling as they cried out prayers for the children.

Yule took a deep breath of the cold air and lifted his head to the heavens. Stars peeked through openings between low-hanging clouds. Any moment now... The sun need only dip below the horizon.

The first peals lifted into the sky, a magical moment that made tears prick in Yule's eyes.

Ro let out an excited yell and began to ring his own bell vigorously. Yule smiled at him. Looking at his grandson's earnest face, his heart squeezed with affection.

Oh, wolf-god damn his earlier lack of

charity and compassion. Yes, if Jason had gone the surrogate route as Yule had wanted, he might have had several more grandchildren, but he wouldn't have had *this* grandchild, now would he?

Yule held Ro's hand more tightly, ringing his stick of bells and listening to the chants from the priests offering prayers for the children, proclaiming the coming of winter-fox, and exalting the miracle of light in winter. Ro's eyes grew more fervent, and his mouth moved with the chant. Yule smiled to see Ro's silent but devout respect for the priests' prayers.

Yule lifted his gaze to Miner's and found his love's smile directed at Ro. Yule felt rebuked for ever having advocated for a world where this young man wouldn't have existed. How could Yule have ever wished for anything to be different when Ro was so precious and loved? He couldn't, and he regretted that he ever had.

Yule lifted his eyes to the sky, his heart

asking for forgiveness from wolf-god, as he rang his bell harder while the tender night descended.

CHAPTER SIX

VALE

THE BELLS RANG outside the house and inside his body, echoing, tingling, chiming, and rising hot, hot, *hot*. Vale was on fire, and it was holy.

Divine. Agony. Bliss.

Nothing could quench his need, not even Jason moving inside him, on top of him, next to him, with him. Always with him.

"Jason!" he cried, climaxing again, his body wracked with pleasure. "Please," he begged. "Please, please, *please* give me a baby! I need it." His voice hitched with a sob. "I need it so much."

Jason thrust into him harder, his hips snapping with such force that plaster drifted down from the hole the headboard had punched into the drywall during the last ferocious round of Vale's heat. The grittiness of the residue coated their slick skin until each thrust of their bodies was rough and raw.

"Shh," Jason soothed, fucking into Vale harder, glistening with sweat, his blue eyes nearly black, pupils blown wide with lust. "Shh, baby. I've got you."

Vale writhed, aching with a brutally hard desire that no orgasm seemed to soften. The wet sounds of their bodies coming together, the bells from the street, all their urgent grunts, and his own pitiful cries gathered like a fist in his heart, hurting like nothing ever had. It needed to release, or he'd die. He'd collapse under the yearning's weight or be smashed in its strength.

Vale clawed down Jason's back, seeking

liberation from the prison of his needful body, scratching his way out of the wild pleasure-pain that consumed him. His hole was sloppy wet with his own juices. His womb was descended and open, and the head of Jason's cock plunged into it with each snap of his hips, leaving Vale quaking with gushing orgasms and screaming with pleasure, and yet it wasn't enough. His body yearned for more. For the thing it couldn't have.

"I need it," he cried again. "I need to be filled with your babe. Please. *Please*, Jason, please."

Jason hushed him again, working his hips so that Vale's glands were milked relentlessly by his thrusts.

"Just one more," Vale whimpered. "Let me have just one more. I need it. So much. It *hurts*. I need it. Please, Jason, *please*. Just one more baby. I need it."

Another shattering peak arrived and passed. Vale collapsed with it, shaking and quivering, all the world reduced to flesh and breath and this endless, brutal need.

Pleading for relief that wouldn't come.

JASON

THE HEAT WAS rough going. Jason hadn't seen such hard and long-lasting crests in all the years he and Vale had been together so far. As he panted in the darkness, the bells having stopped ringing hours before, he hoped for a short reprieve.

His last knot had deflated less than ten minutes before, and Vale had passed out into a sleep so deep that Jason kept checking to make sure he was breathing. An omega couldn't die from heat, could they? Not one as healthy as Vale, surely. And yet he checked Vale's breath again, relieved to find it steady, if somewhat shallow.

At times, Jason felt it nearly impossible to resist Vale's pleas, and yet he held strong. To remove the condom, to fill his womb with seed, give Vale another child? He couldn't risk that. It'd been dangerous enough to deliver Ro, and Jason would never risk Vale's life again.

Still, his own cells cried out to complete the reproductive act. He, too, felt strangely unsatisfied by this mockery of pressing flesh into flesh without creating anything new. He felt sick with need and desire to plug Vale with his cock, to fill his womb with his cum, and know in his heart that he'd put his child inside him.

The conflict between instinct and logic grew with each iteration of the swells of heat.

But Jason would master it. He wouldn't give in.

After making sure that Vale was still sleeping—and breathing—Jason rose from the bed and pulled on his robe. He stumbled down to the kitchen on rubbery legs, exhaustion from the long days of sex making him sway like a drunk as he warmed up a meal. He'd fed the broth of the soup to Vale earlier but knew Vale wouldn't take much more. An omega's digestive track slowed during heat for obvious reasons.

But Jason was famished, though nearly too tired to eat. He pushed meat and bread down his throat and swallowed as much water as he could manage. Then he heaved himself up to go into the library. He wanted to make a few phone calls before the next swell came on, so he needed to do it quickly.

As he sat down at Vale's desk, he pondered the glinting decorations out in the yard. How far away the afternoon seemed when he and Ro had bedecked the yard in anticipation of the arrival of winter-fox. Now it took most of his brainpower to understand that the bells he heard at night weren't some joyous blessing from wolf-god raining down on his shared bliss with Vale.

How many nights had passed? Had it

been five already? Or only three?

Jason dialed the number he'd committed to memory as a small child and hoped it wasn't too late to call. Belatedly, he sought out the arms on the clock and was pleased to see it was early in the evening yet. Ro should still be awake.

"Sabel-Hoff," his father barked.

"Father, it's me. I wanted to check in."

"Jason! Ah, son, is everything going as it should? You're staying strong?"

"Yes, it's all right. I'm eating."

"I didn't mean with regards to the food. I remember how hard it can be to resist the urge to… Well, you know…"

In fact, Jason knew his father had *not* been able to resist at all due to his pater's allergy to condoms and his father's natural inclination and drive to make his pater's heat pain stop. Only *that* had led to a different, just as horrible pain, and now to his pater's sickness…

He didn't want to think about all of that,

but it was a good reminder to stay firm even when Vale was shaking and pleading and wailing for a child.

"I'm staying strong there, too, Father."

"Good, good. I suppose you'll be wanting to speak with Ro?" He seemed to move the receiver away from his ear, and Jason heard him call out, "Ro, your father is on the phone for you."

The sound of running feet and his father's chuckles came down the line before the breathless, "Father?"

"Hi, sweet boy. How is the holiday going so far?"

"It's good. Grandfather really is such a good cook. We've been making all kinds of things for the feast and putting them in the freezer until the right day, which is in just two days now! Tomorrow night winter-fox will come..." His eager voice became quieter. "Is Pater all right? Is he still...is it still happening?"

"He's resting, but it'll be over soon

enough." Or Jason hoped it would, anyway. He wasn't sure he could keep up the pace for more than another day or two. What if this heat dragged on too long? It was hard to know anymore what to expect from Vale's heats. They came unexpectedly, and this one was so frighteningly rough. "He'll be happy to see you in a few more days. So will I."

"I miss you both," Ro said, his voice shaking a little. "It's not the same without you. It's different. And I think I…"

"You think what?"

"I don't know. I'm just worried."

"I know you are, but you don't need to be. Pater is just fine. I promise."

"All right."

"And I know you miss us, but these are special memories you're making with your grandparents. Later, when you're older, you'll be glad for them."

Ro made a soft sound that Jason chose to interpret as agreement.

The clock chimed the hour. "I just wanted to hear your voice," Jason said. "I should go now."

"Does Pater need you?"

"Soon, he will, and I have a few things to deal with before that. Don't worry, all right? Everything is wonderful here. I love you, Ro-ro."

"I love you, too, Father."

After they hung up, Jason wondered if he shouldn't have spoken to his pater as well, but he shoved that aside and hastened to dial the next number. He had to look it up since he didn't have it memorized, though he should have, given the number of times he'd needed to dial it over the years.

"You've reached the Heelies-Riggs-Chase residence!" a beta servant chirped. "How can I help you?"

CHAPTER SEVEN

MINER

"WHAT DO YOU hope winter-fox will bring?" Yule asked Ro just as Miner stepped out to join them on the front porch for the last night of the bells.

Miner had wrapped himself in a heavy coat, and he wore a fur-lined cap that Yule had brought home for him the day before. The air was frigid and smelled of snow, though no flakes had fallen yet. He'd had a hard time breathing most of the day, and his chest felt leaden. He'd smiled throughout dinner, though, hoping to cover how shallow his breaths were and how tight and hot his skin felt.

This was the last night before the Feast of Winter's Heart. They'd enjoyed their time together so much. The days of baking, playing, and decorating, the nights of reading by the fire, or listening to music, or just cuddling on the sofa with their one and only grandchild had been so perfect. There was no way Miner was going to let anything get in the way of this last, beautiful memory being made. Not even the alarming sense that something was truly, absolutely *not right*.

"Well…?" Yule prompted Ro again. "Surely there's something special you hope he will bring."

Ro squirmed slightly. "I just want to hear the bells. I don't care if I get anything."

"What a change from last year," Miner observed, though it was a little hard to speak. Yule didn't seem to notice, though, which was good. If he had any idea how strange Miner felt, he'd be on the phone with his list of doctors' numbers insisting someone come over immediately.

"Indeed. Back then, you had a list of present requests the length of my arm," Yule teased.

"Things change. I'm getting bigger," Ro said with a haughty sniff. "Soon, winter-fox won't visit me anymore."

"That's true." Yule met Miner's eyes and smiled. "Good thing you're still little enough. I bet he's got a lot of things in his magic pouch for you."

"Does he?" Ro asked, brightening a little, eagerness creeping into his voice. "Like what?"

"You'll have to see tomorrow."

Before long, the parade started again. The priests came pouring from the church, the bells rang high into the night, and the peals seemed brighter and sharper than Miner ever remembered. He closed his eyes, focused on his breath, and then coughed.

And coughed.

He turned from Yule and Ro, coughing

into his handkerchief. It went on and on, wracking his throat and bringing tears to his eyes. It didn't stop, not even long after Yule's hand thumped his back, and his low tone worried aloud by Miner's ear.

Finally, he coughed up something big, and he spit into his handkerchief, quickly closing it and stuffing it into his coat pocket before Yule could see what he'd seen: it was red and lumpy.

It looked terrifying.

Wiping his lips with the back of his gloved hand, Miner turned to his alpha and grandson with a smile. "It's all right. I'm fine now. The bells…"

Were over. He'd coughed through the whole of them.

Ro stared at him with wide, horrified eyes, and Yule looked much the same.

"Oh," Miner said. And then he swooned.

YULE

YULE DIDN'T WANT to leave his *Érosgápe* on the floor of the foyer with their sobbing grandson, but he needed to summon help.

Picking up the phone in his office, Yule's fingers hovered over the numbers for emergency services. An ambulance could take Miner directly to the hospital where they might help him, but…

He remembered the last visit they'd had with Dr. Chase only a few weeks before and the grim diagnosis given at the time.

"There will be questions about the cause of his problems," Urho said. "In his decline, it would be best to rely on me, if possible. We don't want them to notify authorities regarding what they'll find in any samples they take for testing."

If only they'd known the abortifacients, taken for so many years, would linger in Miner's body indefinitely. Urho had said something about heavy metals like mercury and cadmium in explanation of the way the abortifacients had done their damage and why they had stayed embedded in Miner's body to do further harm even once they'd been discontinued for good.

If authorities were notified, that would be the end of everything. There was no leniency, not even for an already dying man, never for an omega who aborted unwanted babies, and if they were to discover that Miner bore evidence of abortifacient toxicity?

No, it was too dangerous for everyone in the family to allow Miner to be treated by anyone but Dr. Chase.

Yule found the number at the top of his list of doctors and called immediately. Luckily, a beta servant answered after only one ring, and when told of the emergency, he promised that Dr. Chase would be over directly.

Hanging up the phone, Yule returned to where his *Érosgápe* lay and grandson sat on the cold marble floor of the foyer. He picked

Miner up into his arms and carried him carefully up to their room, noting the way his scent had changed, the way his breath labored. A pit of dread formed in his stomach.

"He needs the hospital!" Ro said, trailing him. "At school, they say to call Emergency!"

"Dr. Chase will come to help him," Yule said, his heart pounding and dark spots drifting before his eyes. He must not pass out. He must stay cognizant and aware. He couldn't give in to the terror consuming him.

"We have to call Emergency," Ro said and turned, running back the way he'd come.

"Ro!" Yule shouted. He lay Miner down on the bed as gently as he could and then ran back down the stairs, grabbing Ro just as he put his hand on the telephone. "You cannot call Emergency. Understand?"

"No! I don't understand! Grandpater is…!" He gestured frantically toward the stairs and dove for the phone again.

Yule jerked it out of his reach and

grabbed hold of Ro's hands. "There's no time for this right now. Dr. Chase will be here soon. We have to take care of Miner now."

"But Emergency can—"

"You cannot, *must* not, call for the hospital. There is more going on here than you understand, Ro, grown-up stuff, but this is important. Promise me."

"But—"

"Promise me."

"I promise," Ro said reluctantly, but Yule knew his grandson never broke a promise.

A banging at the front door alerted him to Dr. Chase's arrival. The man must have sprinted over, and by the looks of him when Yule opened the door, he had.

"Xan is coming with more appropriate clothes," he said as he pulled off his coat and quickly hung it in the closet. He wore only pajamas and, aside from his black doctor's kit, untied boots. He kicked those off and then hastened up the stairs.

"He's in the bedroom?" he called over his

shoulder as Yule followed him.

"Yes."

Then his eye landed on Ro, and he asked, "He won't call Emergency, will he?"

"No," Ro said solemnly. "I won't."

"All right. Good. I've got some supplies here, but Xan will bring extra as well."

"Ro, open the door for Mr. Heelies when he comes, all right?" Yule said, pausing only long enough to get Ro's nod of agreement before following Dr. Chase down the hall and into the bedroom he and Miner had always so lovingly shared.

He took hold of Miner's fever-hot hand and kissed it.

Dr. Chase got to work.

CHAPTER EIGHT

RO

R O STOOD NEXT to the decorated tree with tears streaming down his face.

He didn't know who'd done it—Riki's father, Xan, perhaps?—but there were presents from winter-fox beneath the pine's adorned limbs.

All the night before, he'd sworn to wolf-god above that he'd never lie again, that he'd never, *ever* go against the spirit of the law just to save some disappointment. He'd promised he'd do his best to always live as wolf-god intended and to honor his commandments.

Just please, please, please, please don't let

Grandpater die!

But the morning hadn't brought any good news that Ro could see. Not with his grandfather and Riki's family's resident doctor, Urho Chase, still locked in the room with Grandpater, and Xan pacing by the fire.

The presents seemed a curse, wrapped up in shiny paper and all bearing his name in what was supposed to be winter-fox's magical caligraphy, but now was all too obviously his pater's handwriting.

Yes, he was too old for winter-fox. He'd lied by keeping that to himself. His pater was wrong, *so* wrong, to say it wasn't important, that it was a gift to pretend. Because now his grandpater was dying, and it had to be a punishment for betraying the spirit of wolf-god's holy word.

Ro turned on his heel, ignoring Xan's call of concern, and ran up the stairs to his father's old room. He locked the door behind him for good measure, glad he had when he heard the soft call of Xan's voice outside it.

He knew Xan wouldn't bang, wouldn't yell, because that would disturb Grandpater as he lay…

Dying.

Ro's heart cracked in two, like a bolt of horrible lightning had struck it from within. He burst into sobs. The room was too hot, the walls were too close together, and the ceiling was going to come down on him any second.

Throwing open the window, he climbed out onto the roof. There he saw the blanket of snow over the yard and molded around the roofs of the other houses. It shone like a crystalized cloud. He wiped at his eyes, hiccupping sobs, and crawled on his knees to a patch of roof protected by the tree above. He sat balled up, his knees tucked under his chin, shaking with the cold and determined to never, ever go back in.

Not to the sad silence in the halls. Not to the presents mocking him beneath the tree. Not to the misery he'd brought on with his lie.

Ro didn't know how long he'd been outside—long enough that he'd stopped crying, and the snot from his tears had frozen on his upper lip—when the ladder on the side of the house began to shift and sway. Someone was coming up.

Anger pierced him.

How dare Xan climb the ladder? It was for Riki and Riki only. This was their special place.

A weird crash of painful relief hit him when Riki's curly, dark head poked above the roofline, and he hauled himself up and onto the roof. He wore his red cape again and carried a bag on his back that looked stuffed with something rather light in weight.

"Ah, I knew you'd be out here," Riki said. "I told my father so." He crawled on his knees over the icy snow toward Ro and then unzipped his bag, bringing out a hat, and a blue cape that Ro recognized as belonging to Riki's younger brother, Bek. But it fit well, as

Riki slipped it around Ro's shoulders.

"Oh, Viro," Riki said, putting his own arms around him, too, adding to the warmth of the wool cape. "I'm so sorry."

They sat in silence, their breaths tangling up together in a white cloud, and then Ro muttered, "It's all my fault."

Riki whispered, "How?"

The gust of breath against Ro's neck made him shiver. "I pretended to believe in winter-fox even though I knew better, even though the holy texts state it's a holiday just for children, and this is my punishment. Grandpater will die."

"He's been sick a long time," Riki said.

"But not this sick."

"That's how sickness works, believe me. Urho is a doctor, and we see it all the time. Someone is sick for a long time, but when the end comes, it's always fast."

"The end? So it's definitely the end? Your Urho said so?" Ro's eyes filled with tears again.

"Oh, no, no, no," Riki said, enveloping Ro even tighter. "I didn't mean it like that. I just meant it can't be your fault. I pretend to believe in winter-fox every year, and nothing bad has happened to us."

"Yet."

"Viro…"

"You don't know. What if you're saving up bad luck for the future? What if something very, very, *very* bad will happen for pretending to believe so many times?"

"That's absurd. Then every oldest child in the world would—" Riki huffed. "Never mind. Let's not fight." He hugged Ro tighter. "It's cold. Let's get you inside."

Ro thought about refusing, but his butt, feet, and hands were going numb, so he let Riki lead him through the window back into the warmth of his father's old room. He collapsed on his bed, covered his face with his pillow, and waited. For what, he didn't know. For Riki to open the door and let his father in to scold Ro? Maybe. But that didn't happen.

What did happen was Riki sat beside him on the bed and ran his hand up and down Ro's back, humming a tune and saying nothing. Minutes passed, longer and longer, and Ro grew sleepy. He hadn't been able to rest all night, worry eating at him like a worm, and as Riki sang softly, Ro dropped off into a light slumber.

The sound of knocking at his door jerked him awake, panicked and guilty as if by falling asleep, he'd somehow done further damage to his grandpater's health.

Riki rose from the bed and answered, saying nothing as Xan entered with a tray holding steaming bowls of soup. He put it down on Ro's father's old desk and looked around the room with assessing eyes.

"It's almost exactly the same," he said with a small quirk to his lips. Then his gaze landed on Ro. "Ah, little one, don't cry." He strode across the room to pull him into a hug like Riki had done at first. Only he was bigger than Riki, and Ro fit into the space beneath his chin, wrapped in his strong arms. He'd never been hugged by Riki's father before, but it wasn't bad. Xan's arms felt reassuring.

"I have some good news," Xan said.

"Grandpater is all right?" Ro burst out, pulling back to gaze up at Xan's face.

"Well, no, that is, what I mean to say is that I've heard from your father. Jason and Vale will be here soon. The, ah," he seemed to search Ro's face a moment.

"He knows," Riki supplied quietly, sitting down next to them both on the bed and taking Ro's fingers in his own. "He knows all about it."

"Ah, okay, well, your pater's heat has passed, and they're coming now to be with you."

Ro didn't know how to feel about that. Part of him wanted nothing more than to crawl into his pater's arms and cry until he was empty. But part of him was angry.

Stupidly, burningly, ragingly angry. Because wasn't it his pater who'd told him to lie? Wasn't it his pater who'd basically pleaded with him not to ruin the holiday?

Wasn't it his pater's fault, then, if Grandpater died? At least a little?

His heart, so recently soothed by Riki's humming and soft strokes, now broke again, and the wails he'd managed to quell earlier came back.

"Oh, wolf-god," Xan said in a panic. "Where's Caleb?" he asked, looking over his shoulder for his omega and the pater of his children and finding him not there.

"He stayed home with the others," Riki reminded him.

But when Riki put his arms around Ro again, singing and quieting him, it seemed he was a good enough replacement for whatever Caleb would have done. Xan backed out of the room, saying, "Eat the soup. Your parents will be here soon. Urho is still with your grandpater, and your grandfather won't leave his side, but I'm here if you need me."

Ro continued to cry, and Riki said quietly, "It's okay, Father. I'll take care of him. You go wait for his parents."

Xan said seriously, "You have such a good heart. I love you."

Riki nodded and turned his attention back to Ro. "Shh, let me sing that song again." And he sang, softly, sweetly, his hand sliding up and down Ro's back with the most tender, soothing strokes, and, slowly, Ro's tears stopped once more.

"C'mon," Riki said, leading him by the hand to the chair by his father's desk. "Sit. Eat."

Ro managed to get a few swallows in under Riki's caring gaze. It was then he knew, certain as he could ever be, that Riki was the omega for him.

Érosgápe be damned.

YULE

THE WORLD WAS coming to an end.

His world, anyway.

Yule's stomach was empty but churning wretchedly. He'd nearly passed out twice from sheer fear and panic, but he'd held it together, waiting for Urho to tell him something, *anything* certain. There was only so much 'time will tell' that he could take as he watched the doctor push needles into his *Érosgápe's* skin, trying to save his life.

"It's his kidneys," Urho had said early on.

"I thought it was his lungs," Yule had answered back.

"Those, too." Urho had looked so grim that Yule had felt his soul leave his body and slam back in again.

"Will he regain consciousness?" he asked as Urho stuck yet another needle into Miner's flesh and pressed the plunger down. It was the fourth such shot in an hour. Yule sensed the end was near.

"I can't say."

"What *can* you say?" he barked, tears in his eyes.

Urho took hold of his arm. "It's in wolf-god's power now. I've done what I can, but he's very—"

"If you say he's very sick, I will…" Yule gripped Urho's lapel and tried to shake him, but the man was too big, too muscled to be moved. "I need…"

Urho's eyes softened, so full of sympathy and understanding that Yule felt sicker than ever because he knew what that expression meant. "I know what you need. I've been there myself. My *Érosgápe* was…" he shook his head. "But there's nothing we can do but wait and pray."

"When will we know?"

Urho guided Yule back to the chair next to Miner. "When we know."

The hours passed slowly, the black of night morphing into the sun of morning.

Now there were noises in other parts of the house. Wails from Ro, he thought. He should go comfort the boy. But he couldn't make himself leave. What if…what if Miner found it easier to pass on if Yule wasn't there acting as a tether to this earth?

"I'll wait here," Yule murmured. "I'll wait here forever."

Urho hummed a non-response behind him, and the door opened and closed softly as the big doctor exited the room. Yule thought to call him back—what if Miner suddenly needed something?—but then he didn't.

Alone with Miner.

Just the two of them.

Would this be for the last time?

"I love you, darling," he whispered. "You've been—" No, no, it wasn't over. It couldn't be the end yet. He wouldn't say it like that. He mustn't. What if Miner heard his words and thought he was dying? What if he casually drove the life from his beloved with careless commentary? "You are the light in my day, and I am so grateful for you every second. You know how much I need you. Stay here. Stay with me."

Miner's hand flexed slightly in Yule's, and he gripped him tighter. "Don't you go anywhere. I need you with me. I need you, Miner. Don't go."

Miner shivered, and his breath came in a stagger, but he clenched Yule's hand tighter. A reassuring grip or an apology? Yule just didn't know.

VALE

"WHERE IS HE?" Jason asked, breathlessly.

"In your old bedroom," Xan said, motioning toward the top of the stairs while helping Vale take off his coat.

Jason took the stairs two at a time but

paused halfway up to look over his shoulder. "Pater is in my old room?"

"Oh! I thought you meant Viro," Xan said. "Your pater is where you'd expect him to be. Your parents' room."

"So, he's alive still?"

"He was the last time Urho came out." Xan consulted his watch. "That was just a few minutes ago."

Jason nodded, caught Vale's eye, and then turned to run the rest of the way up the stairs, his footsteps falling heavy and fast.

"Ah, thank you," Vale said as Xan took his hat, too, and hung it in the coat closet by the front door.

Vale remembered the first time he'd visited this stately home and the way Jason had taken his coat then. Not that he blamed him for running off now. Time was of the essence, of course. But he did feel cold and lonely, not to mention weary beyond belief after his heat. It was good of Xan to help him divest himself of the extra bundling Jason had insisted on at home.

"He's dying?" Vale asked.

Xan's lips tightened. "I hope not. Urho won't say."

"That's a good sign then."

"Maybe." Vale was surprised when Xan took hold of his arm and guided him deeper into the foyer and then to the stairway. "Urho doesn't like to give false hope, but he doesn't like to deliver bad news prematurely either. The fact that he had me call you both to see if your heat had ended, and to see if you could handle coming over, says plenty, though."

"Indeed." Vale knew Urho would never interrupt a heat, though he was also aware that Urho was somehow possibly partially responsible for the abrupt end to this one. He hadn't had time to ask, though, or to fully understand, but he remembered vaguely, between swells, Jason feeding him a foul-tasting mixture and telling him Urho had sent it and that it would help.

Whatever the case, his heat was finally over, and he felt as though he were walking through a dream—possibly turning into a nightmare—as he let Xan guide him up the stairs and down the hallway to Jason's old room.

Ah, how young Jason had been the first time Vale had seen this sanctuary, this place that had been Jason's first home.

"He's in here," Xan said, knocking lightly on the door. "Riki's with him."

Vale wasn't surprised to hear that. Riki and Ro were incredibly close, and he wondered at times if, once puberty came for them both and ripened their bodies and scents, they would discover they were *Érosgápe*. But as it was, they were just very dear and devoted friends.

Xan pushed the door open, and Vale took in the scene. Ro asleep on the bed, Riki at his side, fingers in Ro's hair, and his gaze focused fondly on the side of Ro's face. Ah, yes. There was something special between these boys. Something tender.

Vale's heart ached with some bittersweet joy and pain he couldn't quite place, but which must go along with being a parent whose only child was determinedly growing up.

Riki looked up, and his eyes brightened for a moment and then dimmed again as he realized that he should leave. He stood slowly from the bed, careful not to wake Ro, and at the door, he whispered, "He thinks it's his fault. For pretending to believe in winter-fox."

"Oh," Vale said, the sound pushed from him like a punch.

"Poor kid," Xan said, putting a hand on Riki's back and tugging him through to the hallway to stand at his side. "Are you all right to get to the bed?"

Vale nodded. He was wobbly on his feet, but he could pass the distance. "Thank you," he said to them both, and he meant it for more than just what he'd witnessed. He hoped Xan knew that he was grateful for everything their families shared between them, even the things from the past which had once made them less than entirely friends. "I'm fine."

"I'll send soup up."

"No, don't worry. I'm fine," Vale whispered.

"Jason will kill me if I don't."

Vale shook his head. "I'll be all right."

Xan took him at his word at that point, and Vale carefully shut the door on his and Riki's retreating backs. Then he crept over to the bed to lie down beside his son. It didn't take too long before the exhaustion took hold, and he fell asleep with Ro beneath his arm.

JASON

PATER LOOKED TERRIBLE.

His skin was sallow, and his cheeks had sunken in, as though he were turning into a skeleton right before their eyes. Father sat in a chair by the bedside, his hand clenching Pater's like a lifeline.

Turning to Urho, Jason searched the doctor's eyes and found they were not entirely hopeless, at least. He nodded toward the door, and Urho agreed to follow him out. The hallway was quiet. Jason peered down to the opposite end toward his old room and noted the door was closed. Hopefully, Vale was comforting their child there and getting rest if he could, too. It was too soon after a strenuous heat to be out and about, but what else was there to do?

Urho cleared his throat after making sure the door to Jason's parents' room was closed behind them. "It's his kidneys. And his lungs. But I think if we can get his kidneys back on course, we can…" He sighed and put his hands on Jason's shoulders. "You must brace yourself. Even if this is not the end, it will be here soon. There will be no long-term miracles. Not like last time. Understand?"

Jason nodded and fought a strange urge to burrow against Urho's chest. He'd long ago set aside his jealousies of the man, but wanting to hug him? So odd. And yet there Urho stood looking solid, real, and honest—a pillar in this painful confusion.

Urho let out a small huff and then dragged Jason into his arms. Jason's eyes filled with tears. How had Urho known? It didn't matter. He hugged his friend and let his tears spill over. Urho patted his back and then released him. "This is hard," Urho said. "This is the hardest part of love."

Jason nodded, quickly batting his tears away. "Does Father know? Or does he still think…"

"He has some hope, but I think he's aware that even if we save him now, there won't be years ahead together. It is going to be brutal, Jason, seeing him like that. But we all must go through it sometime."

Jason let out a slow breath. "What can be done to help with the kidney problem? To give him a little more time?"

"I've already given him injections of everything I know that can help. We can only wait to see if they work."

Jason followed Urho back into his parents' bedroom and, standing behind his father's chair, put his hands on his father's shoulders. There they waited.

And waited.

For any kind of sign.

RO

WAKING UP, RO immediately knew something was different. Riki's scent was long gone and had been replaced by the familiar, beloved scent of his pater. He rolled onto his side, his heart squeezing with a sad twist, to take in his pater's dark lashes pressed against his cheeks and the wrinkles between his brows standing out as he slept with a frown. He smelled like he always did after spending time away from Ro. Now he knew why. Heat. His pater must smell like this after a heat.

Ro scooted closer, wanting to tuck up against his pater's body, but then he froze. He was angry at Pater, wasn't he?

He stared at his pater's eyelids, silky-looking and smooth, as the eyes passed back and forth under them, presumably following dreams. Ro thought about Grandpater, how he'd looked the same. He was sick now and likely dying.

Pater wasn't well either, was he? Even if Father and Grandpater and everyone else on Earth claimed he was fine, Ro could smell how tired and weak the heat had left him. It didn't seem right. It didn't seem normal. But what did he know about normal? He'd just found out about heats a few days back. He'd just found out how terrifying it was to grow up, too.

Ro closed his eyes and tried to sleep some more, but all he could think about was whether he had a right to be angry with his pater. Pater had encouraged him to lie. Well, not lie exactly, but withhold the truth. Ro knew that acting in bad faith to exploit wolf-god was…

It was…

He shivered. He'd done this. No matter what, he couldn't shake the idea that it was his own treachery, his easy agreement to lie and pretend, that had led to his Grandpater's sudden, sharp decline. Yes, he'd been sick a long time, but he'd been laughing the morning before. He'd been fine over breakfast and happy at lunch. What had changed? Only that the night of winter-fox had arrived, and Ro had still not been honest.

"Love, he was sick long before you were even born and has only grown sicker. This isn't because of you," Pater said, opening his eyes, his voice tired and gravelly with sleep.

Ro frowned. Could he trust Pater? After all, it was Pater who'd suggested they pretend to believe…

"Ro, I'm sorry," Pater said, heaving himself up to a sitting position. It seemed to take so much effort. "I'm sorry for everything."

Ro sat up, too, cross-legged on the bed next to his father. He scrubbed at his face. "What's everything?"

"Well, I'm sorry that I wasn't the one to tell you about heat and babies," Pater said. His green eyes gleamed sadly. "I suppose I knew it was time, but I wanted to pretend you were a baby for a little while longer."

More and more, Ro was starting to think that pretending was a bad idea. Forthright-ness, honesty, truth, all of that had to be better than pretending just so things would be easier. Because they weren't easier, were they?

Pater asked, "Do you have questions about that? I'm here now if you need or want to ask."

"Why wouldn't Grandfather let me call Emergency? He said I mustn't, but you've always said that's the first thing I should do if someone's sick or hurt."

"Ah, well, that's a bit complicated."

Ro gritted his teeth, feeling certain that his pater was going to try to obscure the truth from him again.

"But I'll tell you."

Ro loosened his jaw and listened as Vale explained his grandpater's history with heat, pregnancies that could have killed him, and the final miscarriage that had resulted in his womb being removed surgically. "But the old abortifacients he took did too much damage and remain toxic in his organs. That's why he's so sick."

It all sounded horrific to Ro. Every last

part of it. Heat, pregnancy, abortion, and sickness. What was wolf-god's plan with all this pain and suffering around making babies? All this loss of control and primal drive?

"Do you have any questions about this, Ro? About your grandpater or heat or how babies are made?"

Ro shook his head.

"If you change your mind later, you can always ask your father or me anything at all. We'll be completely honest with you."

"*Now*," Ro said pointedly.

Pater pondered him for a few moments, his eyes seeing through to Ro's anger. He bit his lower lip and sighed. "I'm also sorry that I encouraged you to go against your conscience about winter-fox. I was selfish. And, in the end, even if you come to understand that it had nothing to do with Grandpater falling so sick, you will always make a connection between that and me as the one who insisted."

"You insisted, but I gave in," Ro said, lifting his chin. "Wolf-god says temptation is eternal, but resistance is individual, and so I'm to blame."

Pater tilted his head. "Where did you read that?"

"In the Holy Book of Wolf." He pulled it out from beneath the pillow. "It's long but very informative. Have you read it, Pater?"

"I've read it, yes. A long time ago."

"I'm going to read the whole thing," Ro said, and he peered into his pater's eyes as if challenging him to prevent it.

"All right."

Ro fingered the leather spine of the big book and then slipped it back beneath the pillow. "So, see, Pater? It can't be your fault if it's my fault." He pressed his lips together and nodded firmly. "I've decided not to be angry with you about it."

"Ro, it's not your fault either. You simply aren't that powerful."

"Wolf-god says man is as powerful as his

thoughts are pure."

Pater sighed. "Wolf-god also said not to steal his glory."

Ro tilted his head. "What do you mean?"

"If wolf-god has chosen Grandpater's time, isn't it stealing his glory for you to take credit for it? To take what should be a reunion between wolf-god and Grandpater's soul, one planned from the beginning of Grandpater's life while still in his own pater's womb if the holy book is to believed, and make it about you and your conscience is, in my most honest heart, the exact opposite of what wolf-god would want."

Ro pondered his pater's words, wondering if they were more temptation away from the truth, but as he mulled it over, he considered that Pater must be right. Wolf-god made it clear: his plans, his glory.

"I suppose that's true, Pater."

"Then let's agree to put guilt and blame aside."

"Do you think wolf-god ever makes

bargains?" Ro asked.

"What sorts of bargains?"

"Like if I sacrifice something great, he will save Grandpater?"

Pater's eyes cast down, and his expression grew deeply sad. "Ro, love, wolf-god doesn't make bargains, no. Believe me; I've tried to make so many." His voice grew gruff. "I bargained for years. I begged for a reprieve, for healing of a past wound to my body and soul, and—"

"And then you met father, and your pain was taken away."

Pater flinched. He took hold of Ro's hand. "That's not how it works, love. I still have painful memories. There are still things I can never have despite the promises I made and tried to keep to wolf-god."

"Tried to keep," Ro said, homing in on the weakness in his pater's words. "I *will* keep my promises."

"What bargain are you thinking of making, love?"

"It has to be something big. Something wolf-god would want in exchange for Grandpater's life."

Vale closed his eyes. "It simply doesn't work like that, Ro. Wolf-god isn't mercenary. There is nothing he doesn't have already; there is nothing he could want."

Ro considered his pater's words, but he wasn't ready to give up his plan yet. There had to be something that wolf-god wanted, something that would replace taking Grandpater to be with him.

Vale said nothing more, his eyes going glazed and exhausted.

"Go back to sleep, Pater," Ro said, covering him with a blanket. When his pater had fallen asleep, Ro rose from the bed.

He climbed back out onto the roof to have a good think. He wasn't as smart as Riki or half the kids in his class, but he could figure this out. He knew he could.

The day grew colder, and a few snowflakes fell from above.

Grandpater was wonderful. He was good, smart, loving, and smelled sweet, like good bread. Whatever Ro gave up to wolf-god would need to be as wonderous as Grandpater himself.

There was nothing in his room at home that was half as valuable or wonderful as Grandpater. But the more he thought about it, the more he became certain there was no item, no amount of money even that could be enough.

It would have to be something personal. Something that would really hurt to relinquish, just like it would hurt to let go of Grandpater. Something of infinite value to him.

Riki.

Ro chewed on the inside of his cheek, remembering his promise to Riki to be his alpha, to handle his heats. Would wolf-god be angry if he went back on that promise and made it into a lie? Wouldn't that be just as bad as lying about believing in winter-fox?

Wolf-god had made it clear: keeping a vow was paramount in determining a good man.

But what if he did keep his vow? But backward?

What if he found his *Érosgápe*? Then it wouldn't be a broken promise. They'd always said "unless they find their *Érosgápe*," hadn't they? Ro could offer up his love for Riki to wolf-god in exchange for Grandpater's life.

The thought of not having Riki as his omega, of not ever getting to kiss his mouth or proclaim to the world that Riki was his omega, felt like a knife to his heart. He ducked his head to his knees, letting the agony roll through him, praying.

Would this satisfy wolf-god? If wolf-god saved Grandpater…then he'd know.

If you'll accept my bargain, please save Grandpater. I can't break my promise to Riki, but I swear to try my hardest to find my Érosgápe, *and, when I do, I'll give up Riki to another alpha who will love him. Is this a fair price?*

As he waited in silence with snow landing on his hair, a peace settled over him.

Wolf-god agreed to the exchange.

Ro believed.

MINER

MINER'S STOMACH AND head hurt, and he felt as though his mouth were made of dried-out seaweed. He stirred, and a creaking sound came from right next to his head. Fingers cradled his skull and lifted his head enough that a straw slipped between his parched lips. He swallowed the water gratefully and sighed, exhaustion coming over him again.

"Miner?"

"Father?"

The voices sounded very far away, but Miner pried his eyes open. Haloed by light, his *Érosgápe* and son stood over him. They were so beautiful.

He smiled.

CHAPTER NINE
VALE

THE SABEL-HOFF LIVING room was the way it had always been, except for the large, gloriously adorned tree smack in the middle of it. Vale had never seen the place decorated for Winter's Heart festivities, and he was somehow simultaneously touched and a little bitter to find his in-laws had, of course, gone completely overboard for their sudden, impromptu feast plans.

Beneath the tree were the presents that Vale had wrapped for Ro. They should have been torn open this morning amid shouts of joy and sparkling smiles all around. Instead, they sat neglected and glittering alone beneath the lowest boughs.

Riki and Xan were still waiting with them, and Vale was grateful. He didn't have the energy to be useful, and Riki kept Ro distracted for the most part while Xan ran whatever little errands anyone needed. Including bringing a pot of healing tea and some strengthening crackers to Vale in the living room.

"I'm sure you need to get home," Vale protested as Xan handed over the plate and steaming cup. "Caleb must be missing you, and the children will be anxious to start the feast."

"They'll go on without us," Xan said. "And there will be more feasts."

Vale nodded, taking a sip of the healing tea and turning his gaze to the boys who sat in a corner, holding hands, poking through a set of maps of the Old World they'd found in Yule's library earlier.

"This is our last one," Vale said as Xan

took a seat on the sofa across from him. "Your youngest is, what, six months old now? You'll have feasts for years ahead."

"Yeah," Xan agreed. "Caleb wants another, but I think we are done."

"Oh?"

"Caleb would have babies until he died." Xan winced, clearly regretting his choice of words for many reasons. "He's not bouncing back as quickly these days. Sam was—"

"The five-year-old?" Vale clarified. "Urho's son?"

Xan raised a challenging brow, and Vale lowered his eyes, refusing to engage on what was clearly a contentious issue. Everyone with eyes knew the child was of Urho's seed. But more to the point, Vale and Jason knew that Xan and Urho were in love and that Caleb was asexual and aromantic and loved them as family only. *And* they also knew that Urho and Xan handled Caleb's heats together, as a team, and, well, if Urho had ended up being the one to knot Caleb at some point during the heat that led to Sam's birth, so be it.

But, fine, if Xan wanted Vale to play along and pretend that Sam was his by seed as well as by heart, then they would.

"Sam was a big baby, and Ray's birth was hard. Since then, Caleb has been…" Xan's eyes grew worried. "Delicate. Urho says he needs to be satisfied with the five we have, but Caleb is stubborn."

"He's still young," Vale pointed out. "Maybe after a few years rest…"

"Perhaps, but I'm content for Ray to be our last." His expression grew a little contrite as he admitted, "I'd wanted Sam to be Urho's, you see. He wasn't an accident."

"And Caleb wanted that, too?"

"Of course."

Vale nodded. He believed that was true. Caleb adored his alpha's lover and would want to have his child. "There will be talk. There *is* talk."

"We all knew that going in."

"And how will it be handled?"

"He's my son," Xan said firmly.

Vale nodded and sipped his tea before saying, "Yes, he is your son."

Xan smiled.

The door to the library opened, and all heads turned that way. Xan was probably the only one in the room not disappointed that it was only Urho, coming in to kiss Xan and hug Riki and grab some tea and some crackers.

"How are things?"

"He woke for a moment," Urho said.

"Just a moment?"

"Only just," Urho quickly ate and scarfed down the tea, kissed Xan again, and left the room.

"Waiting sucks," Xan said, and Vale laughed, memories of a much younger, sassier Xan coming to mind. The one who'd hated him.

"It does," Vale said. "For what it's worth, if I have to wait, I'm glad to be waiting with you."

JASON

"I DON'T WANT to scare him," Pater croaked.

Jason adjusted the pillows propping his pater up in bed, and said, "I think not seeing you is scaring him more at this point."

After a few moments of adjusting the bedclothes around his still very fragile pater, Jason opened the door and ushered Ro into the sacred space.

It was just the three of them.

Father had gone to sleep in one of the many, typically unused guest rooms to not fall apart from exhaustion. Vale was sleeping in Jason's old bed, trying to recover from the heat ordeal and his anxiety over Miner. Xan and Riki had gone home for good, and Urho had gone with them, promising to return after dinner to re-evaluate Miner's situation again and stay longer if necessary.

Miner was absolutely not out of the woods. From the morning of the Feast of Winter's Heart until now—four agonizing days—he'd watched Miner rise and fall in health. Ro hadn't been allowed in the sick room until now. Given the wide-eyed expression and the shiny swell of tears, perhaps Miner was right, and it was too scary for him. But Miner could have a relapse at any time. He was conscious, cognizant, and possibly the best he would ever be again. It might be Ro's last chance to be with his grandpater.

"Darling," Pater said with a fragile smile.

Ro shrank back, but Jason held him steady from behind, hands on his shoulders.

"Did wolf-god save you?" Ro asked softly.

"He did," Pater confirmed. "I felt him close by, could almost sense his teeth, but then he retreated. He said I wasn't ready yet."

"Why not?"

"There's a little boy, he said, that had a concern."

Ro's back went stiff. "He said that?"

Jason wanted to warn his pater away from scaring Ro, but Miner went on before he could get a word in.

"He was warm," Pater said, his voice rattling oddly. "He felt golden. Did you know he's golden, Ro?"

"Like the sun?"

"Just like the sun," Pater agreed. He put out a hand, and Ro stepped forward to take it. "He loves you, Ro. We all love you."

"I love you, too, Grandpater." Ro moved closer and then up onto the bed when Miner patted it, inviting him up.

"Don't get too comfortable," Jason said. "Grandpater needs his rest."

"What I need is this sweet boy," Pater said.

Ro snuggled up to Pater's side, and Jason sat on the side of the bed holding their hands. "I was scared, Grandpater."

"So was I, love," Pater whispered. Jason's heart clenched. "So was I."

VALE

RO COULDN'T BE persuaded to open the gifts from winter-fox, even days afterward, and Vale told Jason to leave them alone. He decided to rewrap the presents and give them to Ro as a surprise sometime in the summer when the dread of all this had worn off.

Urho entered the living room and sat down across from Vale. His old friend was growing older by the day, but he was still handsome, what with his salt and pepper curls against his dark skin. He'd been a good lover in their younger years, and Vale was glad he had happiness with Xan and Caleb now.

"How are you feeling?" Urho asked

gently, and Vale was relieved Jason was upstairs with Ro and his parents because the tender expression on Urho's face, especially so soon after a strenuous heat, would set off Jason's possessive streak, even after all these years.

"Tired. Worried." Vale smirked slightly. "Satisfied, but definitely not interested in going through it again soon."

Urho reached out and took hold of Vale's hand, squeezing gently. "Jason called me during the heat before things went bad for Miner. He asked me to look into a few things."

"Oh?"

"The news is good about the new heat suppressant. It seems like the priests are leaning toward approving it."

"Really?" Vale clutched Urho's fingers. He refused to get his hopes up, but a heat suppressant that stayed firmly in his system, good for six months or more, one produced with new science that showed a lessened chance of rebound heat…

"High Priest Garity has a brother, an omega, who suffers from nymph—ahem, I mean, interminable heat."

"High Priest Garity? Wasn't he just promoted to that position last spring?"

Urho nodded. "He's young. Well, younger than most of the priests. He sees things a bit differently. For example, he doesn't believe it's a moral failing or an indication of wolf-god's displeasure that his brother suffers. He believes it's a biological issue. And, of course, if this implant could help his brother, he'd like to see it approved."

"I'm sure he could side-step approving it for the general population of omegas while still helping his brother."

"Perhaps. But he seems inclined to make it more widely available than originally believed possible. Rumor has it he's looking at full availability to all omegas, but, at a minimum, to those omegas who can present a doctor's note showing an interminable heat diagnosis to the degree it puts the omega's life at risk."

Vale's head spun. "How would the implant work?"

"It would be inserted beneath the skin—"

Vale winced.

"It's relatively painless. Just a pinch."

"You say that about those shots you administer, too, and they always burn like wolf-god's spurned lover."

"This won't burn. It'll be subdermal, meaning it will reside under your skin, dissolving slowly over the course of nine months. At which point, they would require a heat to come on before he could insert a second implant. This implant works by changing the hormones produced by the omega's own body, rather than simply destroying the hormone like the prior suppressant. That just made some omega's bodies create more hormones to override it, and, boom, that led to rebound heats."

"This medication would encourage my

body to simply make fewer heat hormones?"

"Yes, and to regulate them so that they occurred in enough strength to trigger heat only when the implant completely dissolved."

"What's the long-term effect of that?"

"Obviously, that's still relatively un-known, but the testing they did on a small sample of omegas suffering from intermina-ble heat and a few others with similar problems as you've been facing was good. They are *healthier*, actually than before, without being overrun by heats…" Urho cleared his throat. "We do know the long-term effect of heats like this on your body, Vale. It will wear you down. Age you faster. Jason needs you for a longer time than that. So does Ro."

The door to the living room opened, and Jason walked in. His eyes darkened seeing Vale so close to Urho, but then he rolled his eyes at himself and advanced with a smile.

"What has my *Érosgápe* looking so wor-ried?" Jason asked as Urho rose from the sofa and moved to a chair next to Vale instead, leaving the space for Jason to occupy—which he did. He took up Vale's hand as if replacing the heat from Urho's palm with his own.

"He was telling me about the new heat suppressant," Vale said, leaning against Jason and taking comfort in his strength and warmth. "It seems the priests might actually approve it."

"Vale is a good candidate."

"How does it work?" Jason asked, and Urho explained it again. "So, he'd still have heats, but not as frequently?"

"And probably not as intensely. He's confided that in recent years, even you've had trouble meeting his needs."

Jason bristled, but then he sighed and let it go. "They get more brutal every time. I worry for him. This last time…there were times I was afraid…" His eyes filled with tears, and his throat worked.

Vale squeezed his hand. "I'm all right.

I'm right here."

"He would collapse between waves. His breathing would grow so shallow. I was scared…" Again he cut off.

Vale inhaled sharply.

Jason stayed quiet, though, and Vale looked up at him, shocked to find that a tear was now slipping down his cheek. "I was really scared…" he said softly. "I didn't want you to know, but…"

Vale hugged him close, and Jason breathed in the scent behind Vale's ear, his frame shaking slightly.

"What if the heat suppressant works like it's supposed to, but when you go off it…there's a rebound heat, and it's even more intense than what we've been dealing with, and what if…" He choked. "What if your body can't take it?"

"That would be a valid concern, but this implant works differently," Urho said and explained that aspect of the medicine to Jason.

"I wish I'd stayed more involved with science," Jason said. "After Ro came, I just wanted to be home with him and Vale when my work at Father's company was over, but if I were still working with a lab, I could see the studies for myself."

"I can get copies for you."

Jason nodded. "That would be great. Not that I don't trust your medical opinion. I just need to read them for myself. For Vale's safety. For my comfort."

"I would feel the same way."

RO

"I HAVE TO tell you something," Ro said, his stomach churning and tears pricking at his eyes. "It's about a promise I made to wolf-god."

Riki looked up from the map of a place

that had once existed called Uzbekistan and nodded. "All right."

Ro swallowed hard. He was a little afraid to admit it out loud. For one thing, it sounded so foolish, didn't it? But for another, Riki was so pretty, and he had such clear, trusting eyes, and he believed in Ro, and Ro desperately wanted to kiss his rosebud lips, and… He supposed it was true; if he kept growing up, his body would betray him, and he'd long to stick his penis in Riki's butt, which was so gross.

But he'd never stick his penis in Riki's butt now.

"I promised wolf-god that, if he saves my grandpater, when I grow up, I'll do everything in my power to find my *Érosgápe*, even if I have to search for years." He kept out the part about having offered his forsaking of Riki as the price. Somehow, he thought Riki would be angry to hear that, and the last thing Ro wanted was to have doubts about his decision.

Riki's eyes flashed with hurt for a moment before he ducked his head and bit into his lower lip. "I see. Thank you for telling me."

"But if I don't find him, I'll keep my promise to you," Ro added, unable to prevent a swell of hope that wolf-god would want that outcome for him instead. That he'd allow Riki to be Ro's after all.

"I know you will," Riki said, but his voice sounded small.

"Don't be mad. Please? You know wolf-god created *Érosgápe* mates as two souls cleaved apart, and it's our duty to look for them." And stick by them, and mate with them, and grow families with them. Wolf-god would show him what he wanted Ro to do. If Grandpater lived, then he'd know for sure. "It's not that I don't want to contract with you, Riki," he said more softly. "I've always wanted that."

The hardest part of this bargain with wolf-god was imagining a future where Riki was not his future mate. Ro had been half in love with Riki his whole life. He was so handsome and smart, and being near him felt like the most natural thing in the world. He wanted to be near Riki forever. Not that he wanted to do the penis-in-butt stuff with him yet, he most definitely didn't, but if he *had* to do it, if he absolutely *must*, then he'd rather it be with Riki. There was no way his *Érosgápe*, whoever he might be, would ever be as wonderful as Riki was in every single way.

Maybe Riki was his *Érosgápe*? His pater said he wouldn't recognize his mate until he'd presented, which was why they took omegas away to boarding school as teens—to keep them safe from early imprinting from alphas.

But what if Riki was his *Érosgápe*? What then? How could he keep his promise to wolf-god in that case? He breathed through the sudden panic.

"Viro?" Riki asked, squeezing his hand. "If you don't want to—"

"I do want to!"

"I mean, if you don't want to keep this promise you've made to wolf-god, whatever it is exactly, you can still back out."

Ro frowned. "And let Grandpater just die?"

"You aren't that powerful," Riki said.

Ro remembered his pater had said the same earlier, too. To wolf-god went the glory. "Wolf-god will do what's right for wolf-god," Ro said slowly. "This is just…it's just a promise I need to make to him."

"But why?"

"Because I have to do something!" he exclaimed.

Ro's eyes softened, and he tugged him forward into a seated hug. "I know. It's all right. I love you, Viro. I love you."

Oh, wolf-god, I love him, too.

And suddenly, Viro didn't know what he wanted anymore. He wished he'd never made his bargain, and yet…

The door opened, and Father strode in.

"Pater's awake," he said with a smile. "He's coming around. Urho says his chances have improved, that we can have hope now."

"He's saved?" Ro asked, heart pounding wildly.

"For now," Father said.

Wolf-god had spoken.

EPILOGUE

RO

P RIEST SHANDALL PUT his hand over
Viro's hair, pushing down against the
crown of his head, and chanted a blessing for
safe travels.

When Viro rose from his knees, he
smiled at the old man who'd become his
advisor and friend these last few years.
Together, they'd traveled far and wide; they'd
sailed to distant shores and climbed
mountains. They'd earnestly sought out
Viro's *Érosgápe* while preaching the Holy
Book of Wolf to the people they'd found in
other regions—some had never heard of

wolf-god, and others had simply ignored his love in favor of other faiths.

But now it was time to part.

A week before, Priest Shandall had listened carefully to the details of Viro's recent disturbing dreams, and he'd sighed, saying only, "Viro, you know as well as this old man what those dreams mean. Wolf-god has spoken to you. Why do you refuse to listen?"

"Because I want to devote my life to being a priest," Viro had whispered.

"Yes, but you can do that with an omega by your side."

Viro swallowed. "Yes."

"Tell me, Viro, what are you so afraid of?"

"I don't know that I want to…that I can…"

"That you can be a good alpha to an omega? Of course, you can! You'll guide your contracted mate to be a strong, moral person just like yourself."

"I don't…I've never…"

Priest Shandall tilted his head. "You don't?"

"I've never truly wanted to be with an omega—or a beta—in *that* way, Priest. Not even when I scent one who is going into heat."

"Ah. You can't use the priesthood to escape your life, Viro. Wolf-god has his plans for you. You've made a promise to an omega, and he's been faithful to you. It's time to keep that promise."

The train lurched, and Viro closed his eyes against the bittersweet memory of parting from the camp he and Priest Shandall had been working in. The clinging hands of the small ones begging him to stay and the backslaps of the alphas, betas, and omegas who wished him a happy journey and a safe one in wolf-god's sight.

The ride into the city took longer than he remembered, probably due to the endless anxiety circling his mind. He'd always loved Riki, always wanted to keep him as his own, and yet…

And yet, being with him the way an alpha was meant to be with an omega had never appealed. But Priest Shandall was right. He couldn't ask Riki to wait for him, to stay on heat suppressants much longer, no matter how often Riki said he didn't mind waiting. Births were always dangerous, but first-time births in older omegas were the most dangerous of all. He owed it to Riki to provide the family he deserved. The family they both wanted.

Why couldn't he make his heart easy with it? Why couldn't he settle into the promise he'd made so confidently and so long ago? Priest Shandall had said wolf-god wouldn't hold him to a promise made in the innocence of youth, but how often had Viro renewed the promise as a grown man? Every letter. Every phone call. And the thought of another alpha being with Riki was…

Viro gripped the armrests of his seat, anger making him go hot all over.

No, Riki belonged with him. No other. So, it was time to fulfill his duty to him.

The train eventually pulled into the station, and Viro was glad he hadn't alerted his parents to his visit, or else they'd have met him at the station and delayed what he needed to do.

He caught a cab toward Riki's family's home.

Viro knew Riki's family in recent years spent all winter in the city and not in the town of Virona since it made it easier for their children to attend their various schools, and they *always* spent the week of the Feast of Winter's Heart together as a family. Viro had no doubt that they would be home when he arrived.

He had the cab driver drop him off at the corner instead of directly in front of Riki's family's home. He needed a few minutes to think and walk and pray.

As he approached the house, he marveled at the wealth around him. Viro was, himself, an heir to a vast fortune, but after spending so much time in the humble lodgings and camps of the priesthood, it nearly dazzled him to see so much glitter and pomp on display.

Viro hesitated at the sidewalk leading to the massive home. It was ridiculously big, inherited from Xan Heelies' father and pater. Viro had been too young to remember a time when Riki didn't live close to his grandparents, though apparently once he'd lived in Urho's mansion when they were not in Virona.

He could see the lights on at his grandparents' house down the street.

Ah.

Viro put his hand over his heart and closed his eyes. The cold air stung his cheeks, and soft flakes of snow fell around him. He breathed in and out slowly, thinking of the last year he'd had with his grandpater before his death. As a grown man, he knew that he hadn't actually bought that year with his childish and desperate vow, and yet...

And yet, he'd still felt in his heart that perhaps somehow, he had. He couldn't let go of that childhood promise, even if he'd used it to shield himself from that which he feared, too: sex. But he'd searched in good faith for an *Érosgápe* he'd never found, and now he was here.

The house was decked out for the holiday, even if there would be no winter-fox and no tree inside and no one to ring the bells, only to listen. Viro smiled to himself, imagining that tonight he'd stand on this porch with Riki—a beautiful, smiling, happy Riki—and hold his hand as the sound of bells rose around them. The perfect circle, the perfect end to his childhood vows.

He'd be proud to be Riki's alpha. He'd find it within himself to do what must be done.

Heart clenching, he stepped toward the front door, climbed the small set of stairs, and rang the bell, waiting for a beta servant to open the door to his future.

His pulse pounded. He felt a little dizzy.

The door flew open, and instantly all of Viro's doubts fell away.

For there stood not the beta servant he'd been expecting, but his own, beautiful, flawless, breathtaking *Érosgápe*. The scent of his flesh was perfect; his skin shone like liquid diamonds; his eyes were pools that Viro wanted to dive into. He saw spots. The earth was the sky, and the sky was the earth. Everything was upside down.

"Oh!" His *Érosgápe* spoke. "Oh, wolf-god, oh, no."

Head spinning, Viro reached for this perfection in human form, and somewhere in the distance, he heard Riki's voice calling his name. Then shouts. And a wail of anguish.

But for him, there was only bliss.

Only the shocked certainty that wolf-god had indeed sent him back to the city by divine hand. Had sent him interventionist dreams to prod him to this exact moment and to the hard, warm body in his arms, the tickle of hair on his cheek, and the pounding heart rattling the breast pressed to his own.

Mine. Always. *Yes.*

The bargain he'd struck all those years ago had been kept.

He'd found home. Completion. Clarity.

No.

He'd found truth.

The truth. And wolf-god alone knew what would happen now.

THE END (FOR NOW...)

Heat of Love Series

"If you're an omegaverse fan, Leta Blake needs to be at the top of your autobuy list. I'm very picky about omegaverse romances, but everything about this series is impeccable—world-building, characterization, complex plots, and incredible sensual tension. Don't miss this one!"

—Annabeth Albert, author of Frozen Hearts series.

SLOW HEAT
- Series Starter
- Age Difference
- Younger Alpha/Older Omega
- Slow Burn
- Heat & Knotting

"Leta Blake is a literary force. Her rich and compelling characters and her dynamic world building, coupled with her skill as a story teller create a magical, one of a kind experience for the reader. The Heat of Love series is the best in its genre."

—EM Denning, author of Upstate Education series

ALPHA HEAT
- Age Difference
- Forbidden Love
- Two Alphas
- Damaged Heroes

"Leta Blake has created complex characters in challenging situations that will break your heart. This books handles some very heavy topics without going truly dark. I highly recommend the entire series!"

—DJ Jamison, author of Surprise Groom

BITTER HEAT
- Hurt/Comfort

- Pregnant Hero
- Forbidden Love
- Heat & Knotting

"Leta Blake has crafted an astonishing story of redemption and the peace that can only be found when you open yourself up to unexpected circumstance. Bitter Heat is a testament to the power of fate and the many different facets of love."

—Kate Hawthorne, author of Giving Consent series

SLOW BIRTH
- Vale & Jason from Slow Heat
- Dramatic Heat & Knotting
- Pregnant Hero
- Pregnancy Sex

WINTER'S HEART

Winter-fox always brings Tristan the best gifts

Tristan wakes every winter holiday to find a present that delights him or teaches him an important lesson.

Learn more about the character of Tristan, *Bitter Heat*'s Kerry and Janus's son, in this short winter holiday-themed story. This small bonus book doesn't contain the heat level of the full-length novels in this series, but it has all the cozy, hopeful warmth for a sweet holiday read. While it ends on a romantic note, the story does **not** contain a romance arc.

This story is **not a standalone** and is best read as an addition to the *Heat of Love* series, preferably after reading *Bitter Heat*. But if you should happen to read it out of order, you can find the rest of the books on Amazon and in Kindle Unlimited.

HEAT FOR SALE
Heat can be sold but love is earned.

In a world where omegas sell their heats for profit, Adrien is a university student in need of funding. With no family to fall back on, he reluctantly allows the university's matcher to offer his virgin heat for auction online. Anxious, but aware this is the reality of life for all omegas, Adrien hopes whoever wins his heat will be kind.

Heath—a wealthy, older alpha—is rocked by the young man's resemblance to his dead lover, Nathan. When Heath discovers Adrien is Nathan's lost son from his first heat years before they met, he becomes obsessed with the idea of reclaiming a piece of Nathan.

Heath buys Adrien's heat with only one motivation: to impregnate Adrien, claim the child, and move on. But their undeniable passion shocks him. Adrien doesn't know what to make of the handsome, mysterious stranger he's pledged his body to, but he's soon swept away in the heat of the moment and surrenders to Heath entirely.

Once Adrien is pregnant, Heath secrets him away to his immense and secluded home. As the birth draws near, Heath grows to love Adrien for the man he is, not just for his connection to Nathan. Unaware of Heath's past with his omega parent and coming to depend on him heart and soul, Adrien begins to fall as well.

But as their love blossoms, Nathan's shadow looms. Can Heath keep his new love and the child they've made together once Adrien discovers his secrets?

Heat for Sale is a stand-alone m/m erotic romance by Leta Blake, writing as Blake Moreno. Infused with a du Maurier *Rebecca*-style secret, it features a well-realized omegaverse, an age-gap, dominance and submission, heats, knotting, and scorching hot scenes.

but he can't help the way he reacts to his touch.

Ned is young, privileged, and hopelessly in love with Ezer. Unfortunately, his pack of so-called "friends" have targeted Ezer for torment. Ned has a lot of regrets, but none greater than his role in Ezer's misery. When Ned's offered the contract of a lifetime, he sees it as the only way to prove he's worthy of Ezer's love.

Too bad Ezer is just as determined not to fall for his bully.

A Bear Shifter Fantasy by Leta Blake

OMEGA MINE: SEARCH FOR A SOUL MATE

Can an Alpha find his dream Omega on reality TV?

Alpha Hank Morrow is a police officer and Alpha bear shifter who has never found the right Omega. Without the steadying influence of a bond with his Omega, Hank's powerful Alpha senses are beginning to overwhelm and endanger not only him, but his fellow police officers and the entire city of White Edge. The chief of police and the governor sign Hank up for a reality TV show to help unmatched Alphas find their dream Omega.

Omega Mine: Search for a Soulmate certainly isn't Hank's idea of a great plan, but he's not given a choice. Now he's off to a tropical island to meet over one hundred potential Omegas in a televised version of hell.

Or is it?

Evan Vaughn is an unmatched Omega. He and Hank have actually met once before at an Alpha-Omega mixer, but apparently he didn't make much of an impression at the time. Will that change on the set of *Omega Mine*? And can anything real come out of a reality TV dating show? Hank and Evan are about to find out...

The Bachelor meets **Alpha-Omega romance!**

This book is nearly 40,000 words of an oblivious bear shifter finally meeting his soul bonded match and a happy ending you'll love! Warning: There is no mfm in this book. There is no ménage in this book. There is no cheating in this book. There is an attraction to someone that is not the other MC but it does not come to fruition.

Gay Romance Newsletter

Leta's newsletter will keep you up to date on her latest releases and news from the world of M/M romance. Join the mailing list today and you're automatically entered into future giveaways.

Leta Blake on Patreon

Become part of Leta Blake's Patreon community in order to access exclusive content, deleted scenes, extras, bonus stories, rewards, prizes, interviews, and more. www.patreon.com/letablake

Other Books by Leta Blake

Contemporary

Will & Patrick Wake Up Married
Will & Patrick's Endless Honeymoon
Cowboy Seeks Husband
The Difference Between
Bring on Forever
Stay Lucky

Sports

The River Leith

The Training Season Series
Training Season
Training Complex

Musicians

Smoky Mountain Dreams
Vespertine

New Adult

Punching the V-Card

'90s Coming of Age Series
Pictures of You
You Are Not Me
Only You

Winter Holidays

North's Pole

The Mr. Christmas Series
Mr. Frosty Pants
Mr. Naughty List
Mr. Jingle Bells

A Boy for All Seasons
My December Daddy

Fantasy

Any Given Lifetime

Reimagined Fairy Tales

Flight
Levity

Paranormal & Shifters

Angel Undone
Omega Mine

Horror

Raise Up Heart

Omegaverse

Heat of Love Series
White Heat
Slow Heat
Alpha Heat
Slow Birth
Bitter Heat

For Sale Series

Heat for Sale
Bully for Sale

Audiobooks
letablake.com/audiobooks

Discover more about the author online

Leta Blake
letablake.com

About the Author

Author of the bestselling book *Smoky Mountain Dreams* and fan favorites like *Training Season*, *Will & Patrick Wake Up Married*, and *Slow Heat*, Leta Blake has been captivating M/M Romance readers for over a decade. Whether writing contemporary romance or fantasy, she puts her psychology background to use creating complex characters and love stories that feel real. At home in the Southern U.S., Leta works hard at achieving balance between her writing and her family life.

www.ingramcontent.com/pod-product-compliance
Lightning Source LLC
Chambersburg PA
CBHW061527310726
48972CB00008B/2347